THE

GAMESHOW

BY

ALEXANDER

RAPHAEL

Opening

It was a funny sort of group that waited impatiently in reception, like errant schoolkids dragged in on a Saturday by their disappointed parents.

An outsider looking in would have immediately become aware that all but one of the group was in their 20s or 30s, most were stylish and photogenic, either from natural poise or just plenty of practice. They might have noticed that four of the six were white, that the group was equal numbers male and female, or else that they were all immersed in their phones and ignoring each other. But most of all they would have sensed the restlessness, the discomfort and the slight fear from six strangers who were used to calling the shots, realising that here in the Office Badlands, they had no authority, control or popularity. Rather than being surrounded by those who were paid to agree, compliment or laugh with them, they were sat as a bunch of former celebrities. People they had never met and yet knew a little of.

The tense atmosphere was offset by the bright and breezy day, on the well-lit and recently furnished waiting room on the eighth floor. It was 10 am, but it would have seemed bright any time of the day. Posters of previous shows were displayed as though trophies. What felt like hundreds of meters up in the sky, they were worth more than any piece of metal. Here in the IPPR TV comedy department, the shows and anyone attached to them were royalty.

The six fidgeted and sat as though the room was hot or the chairs cheap, made more uncomfortable by there being no signal on their phones. The oldest of the group, a well-groomed man in his early fifties, put down the newspaper he had momentarily picked up and looked at the large clock behind the receptionist.

"Have you finished with that?" asked the blonde woman next to him, pointing to the large newspaper he had just folded.

"Sure, be my guest," replied the gentleman with a smile, stroking his pristine moustache. It was good to know young, attractive women were still charmed by him.

Smack!

The man turned to see the tall and elegant woman delighted as she lifted the rolled-up paper from the wall and handed it back to him, with a dead fly splattered within the sports pages. As the man grinned ruefully, the woman, dressed in a pristine orange business suit, flicked her long, blonde, wavy hair back with immaculate poise and got back to the business book she was reading.

"I wonder what's taking so long," asked an in-shape black guy out loud as he stood up. Whether he was talking to himself, the receptionist or to the other five was unclear. He was impeccably dressed in a black suit and red tie, and shoes that looked as though they had been polished at least three times. He was tall, good-looking and broad-shouldered, and used to being listened to, whatever room he was in. When no one replied, he hesitated momentarily before realising he'd be more successful changing tack. "I'd have had a longer workout if I'd known we'd be kept waiting so long!"

"Mrs Stevenson will be out shortly," was the curt reply of the receptionist, who didn't look away from her screen. Working for Selina Stevenson was about mastering the art of looking busy on the rare occasions when there was no work to do. Those were rarer than the steaks Selina would wolf down every Friday. But while the hours were long and the work stressful, the bonuses were fantastic, and the work parties were legendary. Work hard and you could party as long as you wanted.

There was a sudden noise, and the group turned in shock. The youngest, a 27-year-old mixed-race woman with long purple hair tinted within her dreadlocks, had smashed the drinks machine, less in strategy than in anger. It hadn't worked. The bottle of water she wanted was still lingering. She was helped out by the scruffiest of the six, who took his hands out of his pockets and reached for some change.

"Here, take this," he said. "Actually, I'll have a can of coke while you're there," giving her enough coins to get both. She nodded and then repeated the same process again twice, both successfully. She merely grunted while handing him his can.

"Don't mention it," said the unshaven man in a voice full of depth, as though he had handed her a bag of gold. He was curious to know about her numerous tattoos and tempted to make a joke but thought better of it. The woman looked at him slightly oddly but didn't say anything as she sat down moodily.

The remaining redhead sat silently, save for a low hum of a melody she kept repeating in different pitches and rhythms. When she changed to vocal exercises, her southern twang was unmistakable.

It was at that moment that there was a buzz, and the receptionist let them through. The six knew full well that they had been kept waiting for 45 minutes and rushed into the room that had suddenly opened. They were unaware that the woman whose grand office they were entering had been watching them through a camera the whole time and making notes.

Her impressive aura wasn't what they first noticed as they sat down. Instead, it was the vast array of awards and accreditations. Not to mention the photos with two former presidents, three different members of the royal family and one of her on top of Mount Everest. This woman had the success the six had been aiming for and once thought they had been close to getting.

"I know you have a lot of questions, so let me start by telling you a bit more about myself and why you're here," said the refined woman, who couldn't have been more confident in her speech if she had been reading off a screen. She had attended countless courses in public speaking to ensure she was the best and still regularly attended them just to stay sharp. She was in her 50s but maintained a slim figure and skincare of someone 20 years younger through vigorous exercise and a punishing diet. Not to mention all the latest oils, moisturisers and beauty treatments. Appearance was a big part of her job. Her sleek black attire was worth more than the other three women's outfits combined.

"I am Selina Stevenson, Head of the IPPR Network. I'm the one who has the final say if a show gets made. When I started here, the network wasn't even in the Top 10. When I took over as boss five years ago, we were seventh. We are now third."

And she pointed to a chart with dates and figures, covering those 10 years. "According to my latest calculations, we will be top within two years, especially as "Those Krazy Kids" is in its last season. That show has been single-handedly keeping the TPT network in second for years. Being top would mean more than any of the eleven awards I have won. That is what drives me."

None of their questions had been answered, but no one said anything. The 31-year-old guy wearing an ill-fitting New York Knicks jersey counted to check all eleven were there. While he thought he was being discrete, everyone else, including Selina, noticed him scrunch his face as he only counted ten. "The eleventh one is behind you." She smiled and pointed to the one next to various swimming medals and photos of her husband, three kids and two dogs.

"That's context about my role," said Selina as she put the chart away and wiped something off one of the trophies, even though it was already spotless. "Now, three things you should know about me. 1. You will not meet anyone more driven than me. Michael Jordan would be the one asking me to take it easy. 2. I can either be your best friend or your worst enemy. I'll let you decide which side is better for you. 3. I have to be the best and won't accept failure."

Selina looked round the room and observed they were all paying close attention. "Now we come to why you're here. I know you've all had a rough time of things the last couple of years. Let's face it, you've all made some outrageously bad decisions recently. And despite having the most expensive PR teams, you've not been able to fix it. The public has decided they don't like you anymore. And once the public decides you're a joke, you're a disgrace, you're an embarrassment, then you're finished. The thing about being a celebrity is there's no shortage of people willing to take your place with a new backstory, a new look, a new set of skills to win people over.

"But I'm not here to lecture you on your mistakes. Instead, I'm here to offer you a final chance. The opportunity to not just get back to where you were before, but to head from the back of the line straight to the VIP section. From nothing to everything. Discarded trash to jewels in the crown. You six can be so famous those same celebs ignoring your calls will be begging you to come and hang out with them. And to be seen out with you. All the shows, vlogs and podcasts that don't care about you will be offering you everything, and I mean everything, to get you on. So let me explain more about what you've all signed up for."

There was a hushed silence, which the oldest man took to mean they could ask questions. "What is the show called?" he said in a voice as calm as he could make it. "My agent said you were between different ones."

"Ah, we've had the name for a while," said Selina. "It was one of the first things we came up with."

"My rotten agent," he spat out with venom. "The lying piece of sh…"

"Oh, he didn't lie," she responded with a subtle grin. "I didn't tell any of your agents. I just told them enough to get you on board and to get your signatures. But let me tell you more before you ask any more questions," said Selina, keen not to show even the slightest hint of losing control.

"You see, the secret in TV is to give people what they want. Not what they say they want, but what they actually want. Think about it. Those in the media will talk about values and setting a good example, but what do they write most about? Sex, money, violence and controversy. Some people are afraid of taking things to the edge. I don't care if we go to the edge. In fact, I want us to go so far past it, people will be talking about us in their sleep! I don't care what people say. They can do their "Think of the children" routine all they want. To grab bigger ratings than ever before, we have to go further than ever before. This is the future. I'm just bringing it forward. And you are the lucky six to benefit."

She clicked something in her hand and suddenly a projector opened up within a wall and a video started playing, beginning with the network's logo. She paused it for one final message.

"And so, the final explanation of what it is all about. What you've been so desperate to discover. Here is the trailer of your new adventure."

"You thought you knew these celebrities," boomed a deep voice as the six were shown in a dazzling montage. "New York comedic talent Nate Reeder, Tennessee's finest musical redhead Linda Meyes, retired American Football sensation Denzel Harker, trendy Pilates influencer Yasmeen Kahley, political wiz Jed Dexter and heiress entrepreneur supreme Madison Larouch. You've seen their highs; you've seen their lows. Now it's time to see them as you've never seen them before. Get ready for the most controversial of shows, *Wheel of Phobia*."

There were gasps as the mesmerised group was completely caught off guard but couldn't look away from the wheel with their six names on it. Bright, shiny, large, the wheel was big enough to almost touch the already high ceiling. It was spectacular and it was terrifying.

Amid dazzling graphics and a funky musical background, the rules were being explained. "The one, the only, Buck Jackson will be presenting. Each episode he will spin that wheel and whoever it lands on has to face their phobia. No audience voting, no judge picks, no point scoring, it's all done on the luck of the wheel. We've added our own dash of originality to heighten their fears and push them to the limit. Can they handle it?"

And then the video zoomed in on Buck Jackson and his trademark fluorescent suit. "Just like Russian Roulette, only one player will be safe. But who? And who will end up with the grand prize of 7.2 million dollars? Tune in for the first episode on Friday at 8 pm on IPPR 1." The words "Unmissable" showed up in red letters as though fired from a gun, before dissolving in a puff of smoke.

And with that, the screen disappeared, and the lights came back on. Selina had a wide smile on her face. "I thought you'd like that prize! There's nothing on TV even close to it. And what's amazing is that we don't need to worry about any sponsors pulling out. We have mystery backers who will back it even if there are complications. So, people can whine and threaten as much as they like, the show will be going on even if people want to stop it."

There was a stunned silence. The six fidgeted in their seats.

"So only one champ, the rest of the suckers get squat!" said Denzel as he stood up in a dramatic fashion, his eyes narrowing in rage. "That sucks ass!" he shouted as he kicked his seat away. Selina was unruffled but calmly indicated for one of the security staff to put the chair back.

"You're saying only the first person, well the winner, gets anything?" said Yasmeen in bemusement. "The rest end up with nothing. Not exactly fair."

"Sounds entertaining!" said Nate sarcastically. "May as well just chuck us out of a hole in the sky like in *Game of Thrones*!"

"Ah Denzel, you were an elite athlete for 10 years," said Selina, in that same assured tone as before. "You won a Super Bowl in 2012. You know life is about the glory. Doing everything possible to get to that nirvana. You don't get anything without sacrifice. By taking the easy option. You got there by working your ass off every day since you were a kid. And sure, some luck too. You benefited when Shawn Laronda broke his leg during that freak accident three games into the season. When luck came your way, you were ready. You know nothing is just hard work or just luck. It's a percentage of both. I know you're ready for this. You weren't called Maverick for doing things easy!"

She turned to face Nate, who stared at her impatiently. "Nate, you're a season ticket holder at the New York Knicks. Think what influence you could have with $7.2 million! Even if you don't get involved with the board, you'd be able to buy the biggest VIP box and be on first-name terms with all the players. Every time you had a birthday or Christmas party, or even to impress a girl, you could have them all turn up at your front door. Think what your high school bullies would think of you then! Not to mention being able to go on tour again and choose your own venues and support acts."

Selina surprised everyone by slowly going right up to Yasmeen and rolling up her jacket sleeve to show a specific tattoo. "What does this say? I'll tell you. 'When the weight of the world is on your shoulders, crawl on your knees.' And that's what you've done. When life hasn't seemed fair, you always find a way to get through it. When your father told you that your Pilates fitness videos were a waste of time and threw you out of the house for a lack of ambition, you weren't discouraged.

You found a dilapidated studio and after renovating it, soon started filming. When the landlords tried to shaft you with a sneaky increase, you exposed them and ended up helping the other tenants. When rivals started stealing your ideas and your production team, you relaunched with innovative technology and a more loyal team. And got your revenge in a hilarious video. I know you have big plans for making the Piranhas a franchise team and completely changing the view people have of veganism within sports."

The three celebrities were deep in thought. Despite their fears, Selina had been able to tap into each of their wildest desires and make them sound like realistic dreams.

"Well, bravo for them but I couldn't care less about sports," said Madison abruptly. "A bunch of people running around throwing a ball or hooping it 10 feet in the air whatever doesn't interest me. My family and I have sponsored different sporting events and there's always chaos involved."

"Think of it like this, Madison," reasoned Selina. "There is a one in six chance you win without doing anything other than watching a wheel being spun five times. I know you're not short of money. But this will be money you have earnt. You've had an impressive set of entrepreneurial achievements, but you know you'd been unable to escape the family shadow. All those suits who don't take you seriously because of your gender and surname, saying anyone could have done what you did with your family's money. You could shove it right down their throats!"

"What if we decide to back out?" replied Madison, half in defiance, half in curiosity. Selina smiled, impressed with her subtle change of subject and amused at her confidence to take her on. "My agent said it's still possible to cancel if I get col...if I decide I have other ventures to focus on."

"You're a smart girl, very smart," said Selina with a smile so mischievous she may as well have licked her lips. "If you wanted to lose all your money, throw away your career and be blacklisted then yes, it is possible to try. I'm very aware of your wealth. But I have a whole network behind me, plus every major judge, police officer, journalist and lawyer on first-name terms. I could not only destroy you in litigation, I could make you a laughing stock. I had the finest lawyers draft that document that you all signed. Like I said though, you're an intelligent girl and I know you're just making sure. Like a chess player checking the rules again before making the first move."

"I may look fresh-faced, but I'm not as young as these contestants," said Jed in a tone that couldn't hide his pomposity. "If there's some form of American Gladiators assault course then I'm done. I'm going through the door right now with my head held high."

"We are aware of the circumstances of every contestant," confirmed Selina, with just the slightest hint of impatience before she broke out into a smile. "No one will be asked to do something they cannot do. What would be the fun in that? Besides, the challenges will mostly focus on the mental side."

Selina was ready to move them to the room when a voice rang out. "What's my motivation?" cried out Linda Meyes politely in her southern accent. "I don't care about money, or sports or number of followers. All I really care about is music. Not the showbiz stuff with some gimmicky wheel."

"It's not a gimmick," said Selina, with a bemused look. "It's the future. But we'll get more into that later. Who are your musical heroes? Aretha, Whitney, Mariah, Bowie, Diana Ross, Bob Dylan, Taylor Swift, Jeff Buckley. Artists who have transcended their generation and will be played as long as music is played. Your music is majestic, like a nightingale. I listened to *Full On, Max Out* in the car when you released it last year. But no one played it. I bet you none of your five co-stars can name you one song from that album."

Linda looked round in hope but was soon disappointed. From their faces, Linda knew she would get the same response if she asked who she had collaborated with or if they knew what type of animal she'd used for her cover. Her shoulders slumped. She had put so much into it. It had been her most personal work to date.

"Their response was that they hadn't heard it," said Selina with conviction, staring right at Linda. "They never said they didn't like it.

That's why you need to be on a show that will make them listen to your work. And thankfully for all of you, I have created that show."

Selina paused for emphasis. "Three final things to mention. First of all, you'll have noticed there was no signal on your phones. That was no accident. From now on, there will be no contact with the outside world until you are removed from the process. That means you'll need to hand over your mobiles right away. I personally guarantee no one will look at them."

There were grumbles of complaints from the six, dismayed at letting go of something they were so connected to.

"I've got song demos recorded on there," whined Linda in horror. "I haven't made copies yet. You can't make me give it up!"

"You mean, I won't be able to watch any Knicks' games!" cried out Nate in utter dismay. "Not even know the actual results?" he pleaded.

The others were going to say something, but Selina took control of the situation again in her calm but firm voice. "I don't expect this part of the process to be popular with you, but it is necessary. You cannot be aware of what is going on in the outside world. It would ruin everything. I can promise that no one will have access to your phones and that you will adapt."

And with that, the security guards took the phones from all six, Nate's hesitancy to hand his over almost comedically so. They were about to follow them to the safe, but Selina beckoned them not to.

"This leads me on to the second point. Jed, Madison and Nate, you will need to give up your watches. One of the rules of this process is that you won't be able to know what time it is until you have left."

"That would be chaos!" cried out Jed appalled. "I wouldn't know what time to wake up, go to sleep, eat…"

"I know you will get used to it," said Selina in a formal tone, with an expression that didn't betray anything.

"Gonna have to embrace the madness," said Nate under his breath, as he took off his Raphael Ninja Turtles watch with a hint of sadness. He'd had it since he was 10, when he got it as part of a cereal promotion. Jed and Madison reluctantly handed their expensive watches over with ashen faces, fully aware of how difficult a life without order and communication was going to be.

"So how will it work with food?" enquired Denzel. "If we don't know what time it is, how will we know when to eat?"

"Breakfast, lunch and dinner will be available for you at the time you would like it," said Selina as though it was the most natural thing in the world. "There will be a stove for those interested in cooking something, plus a regularly replenished fridge, freezer and larder. There will also be cereals, a toaster and various snacks. We have chefs available who will be able to send dishes up via a dumb waiter."

"I'm guessing they don't have anything much for vegans?" said Yasmeen with a sigh.

"Your dietary preferences and necessities, as with the other five, have been accounted for," responded Selina, mildly surprised that her organisational skills were being doubted. "The list of ingredients will be available on all foods, and vegan dishes will be marked with a blue colour. Should you be unsure, you can write a note and send it down the chute in the kitchen area and it will be confirmed by one of the kitchen staff on call. That's the same method you can use if you require a specific dish."

The six were picturing the different possibilities and problems of not knowing. Selina knew she needed to get her final point across while they were still distracted.

"Third and finally, as mentioned earlier, you won't be able to communicate with anyone from the outside world under any circumstances. You won't be able to call, video chat, send messages or anything. They won't be able to contact you either."

"So if my wife ends up in hospital," speculated Jed, "or one of my kids goes missing or..."

"Under any circumstance," said Selina in a tone that was half offended and half bemused. "Those are the rules. It's too late for any of you to back out, so I suggest you focus on getting your head right before you begin."

And she led them out into the corridor by the elevator, but Denzel did not get in. "I never use them," as his impressive frame walked quickly towards the stairs. "It's all about fitness with me."

A different security staff than earlier accompanied him while the others got in the elevator. Going down seven floors, they entered a studio that was as sleek and modern as you could imagine. They were soon followed by Denzel and the bodyguard, who was even more muscular than him. Neither was out of breath.

"Now you need to get ready for the video room," explained Selina. "We found several outfits for you to choose from, having extensively studied your previous attire. You have 20 minutes to choose what you want to wear. The changing rooms are behind you."

And with that, she was gone. Jed Dexter didn't even look at any of the options. He looked at himself in the mirror, smiled and then sat down to start reading one of the magazines on display. Madison glanced at the outfits, impressed, but after studying herself in the mirror, realised that red really was her best colour and sat down a few seats away from Jed. Denzel came close to changing but despite trying on various different shirts and belts, decided to keep his suit. Linda added a pink scarf. Nate swapped his New York Knicks basketball jersey to one with the slogan "Usually Funny." Yasmeen wasn't impressed with any of the clothes on offer.

Observing them through screens, Selina looked down at her notebook and the circle next to Nate's name she had labelled before they had started looking. No one else had been highlighted. She waited for 20 minutes exactly before joining them again, this time with several makeup and hairdressing staff.

"Okay, let's get going, people," said Selina with urgency and yet in the same composed tone as always. "A quick touching-up session for each of them and we're good to go."

And then there was a whirl of activity like a swarm of bees, with every form of hairspray, fake tan, concealer and everything else that made the group as photogenic as they could possibly get. They were then taken to six different soundproof walls before coming out 10 minutes later.

Before long, they were all ready. Selina stood back to face them; posture so perfect you could have watched a film on her back as though it were a flatscreen. "We're almost ready. There's just time to remind you all of how this game works. This was all explained to you in the contract but I'm going to go over it again."

They suddenly saw the wheel come into place. If it looked imposing on screen, it was even more so when right in front of them.

"As we will make clear, this is not a weekly show. The fact is that it could be a week, it could be longer than a week, it could be on the same day as the previous spin. It all depends on how fast the previous phobia challenge is carried out, among other factors. You'll be given an hour's notice before each new spin though. Within that hour, anything you don't wish to lose must be on the bed or next to it. Anything left in draws or wardrobes will be destroyed. You won't receive your phones back until after you have left the process, or of course, if you're the last player standing."

Selina walked towards the board and spun it, the whirling noise being dominant as though they had walked right past a beach and its glimmering waves rather than the bright studios and sound of several crew getting things ready backstage.

Selina couldn't help but notice the way the eyes swapped from her to the wheel. "You can relax, I'm just demonstrating it!" There were audible gasps of relief.

"Our presenter will be Buck Jackson, and he will always be the one spinning the wheel. Any attempts to share the prize by any form of collusion will not be tolerated and will only get you expelled. Instead of any winnings, you will be forced to carry out the challenge, plus lose all the privileges available to you in the house. And there would be further punishments," she said with a hint of devilry. "But if I explained what they were, that would only sour the mood and make them less effective when carried out."

The wheel stopped spinning, landing on a red strip marked 3. She spun the wheel again and looked up at them. "As you know, there won't be any contact with the outside world until you are out. You will sleep in two separate sections of the building, guys on one side, girls on the other. You're all adults, so any romantic adventures are up to you, but know the cameras will always be on."

Selina could sense the unease of the six and knew further speeches would only lose them. "What else do you want to know?"

Linda went to speak, but Jed interrupted her and went first. "You said no contact with the outside world, and we can't even go for a walk until we're out. What will we do between sleep and challenges?"

"All of your interests and passions have been taken into account. There is a basketball hoop, a batting cage, various different gaming consoles and all manner of games (internet switched off, of course), countless board games, playing cards, books, magazines, a jukebox, a pinball machine, a guitar and a TV that can only be used to watch films and shows filmed before this process began. We also brought some of your personal items to help you feel more at home."

The wheel stopped, this time on a black strip marked 1. Selina started another spin.

"You said the cameras would be filming us all the time," asked Madison, who made sure she got her question in before anyone else. "Does that mean everything we do will go out as live?"

"A very valid question, Madison," smiled Selina genuinely. "To all intents and purposes yes, but not for everyone. Premium package members will get access to 24/7 coverage. Regular subscribers will see the main events, plus summary highlights every night and bonus footage at regular intervals. Non-subscribers will only see the spinning of the wheel and the challenge itself."

"Perverts won't watch us in the shower or on the toilet seat, will they?" exclaimed Yasmeen. "You wouldn't believe some of the psycho fan mail

I've received. One guy once said he'd pay me a grand if I sent him my gym clothes unwashed. And one weirdo actually said he'd marry me if I sent my dirty towel and used handkerch..."

"We get the picture," smiled Selina. "No, no cameras in the toilets, including showers. There will be a rule of only person in a bathroom at any one time, just to avoid any collusion."

The wheel stopped on the number 2. Instead of spinning a fourth time, she moved away from the wheel.

"How do we know this hamster wheel is legit?" asked Nate.

"Before each spin, you will choose a colour at random. That colour will then go down a grid where a number between 1 and 6 is attached. We use every form of technology to ensure the utmost secrecy, reliability and fairness. You've seen me spin the wheel three times; each has landed on a different spot. We couldn't rig it even if we wanted to."

"What made you choose us?" asked Denzel, whose fine physique could be truly admired now he had taken off his jacket. "It wasn't like we applied for it."

"I wasn't exaggerating when I said I knew everyone important in this city," responded Selina, with impressive authority. She hadn't even raised her voice. "I've had countless people examining every aspect of your life. Every relationship you've ever had. Every family member you've ever spoken to. Every colleague you've ever met. You were not chosen by coincidence. You are all here because you are going to make the gameshow the most unmissable programme ever made."

And with that, she opened the doors to the two bedrooms as a klaxon sounded. "The cameras are about to roll. You have an hour before the first spin. Let's rock this!"

And with that, she was gone.

I

Knowing they only had 60 minutes, they rushed quickly to their labelled rooms, the men heading to the left, the women to the right. There was a frenetic energy between them, helped by the knowledge their rooms each had three large beds, three separate showers (with shower caps, hairdryers and every possible type of soap, shampoo and conditioner imaginable) and plenty of space for their things.

"Out of my way!" thundered Madison, as she told herself to keep calm. "Pressure is a privilege," she told herself as she carried the business books to her bed and scanned them with interest for the right chapter to inspire her.

"Be careful!" replied Linda, who was worried Madison would drop the heavy books on her feet. She picked up a guitar that was on one of the beds and, having tuned it to how she preferred it and added a capo on the second fret, played 'Distant Night', one of her earliest hits. "Watch the stars fall from the sky, watch my heart break as I say goodbye," she sang with a confident beauty that was at odds with the nerves she felt. Though it was one of the simpler hits she played, mostly using variations of G, F and C chords, it had always been one of her signature songs. She went to play another, but Yasmeen snatched the guitar out of her hands and carried it to the living room.

Linda didn't say anything, but instead followed her out and on the sofa started playing different tracks from her repertoire. Yasmeen slammed the door on her way back to the bedroom, startling Madison, who went back to reading. Fearful that her new roommate would come back and break the guitar if she was too loud, Linda stopped singing and played quietly. Yasmeen took a deep breath, sat down in the middle of the room and then began to meditate.

Meanwhile in the men's bedroom, Denzel had thumped his chest to get himself going, along with quoting his favourite lines from sporting films, including *Rocky*, *Any Given Sunday* and *Remember the Titans*. He reminded himself he had won a Super Bowl. Unlike the others, he was used to this pressure. Heck, he thrived on it, he told himself. Unsure what to do with all the adrenalin surging through his body, he went to the batting cage and hit some fastballs.

Jed calmly sat down on his bed, as he studied the chaos and wondered if things were hectic in the women's room. The Chicago native reminded himself that he was being filmed and would have to keep his emotions in check. The more he kept himself hidden, the more secrets he could reveal in his book. Jed didn't care what he had signed. He would find a loophole. He always did.

Nate was using one of the blank notebooks, making sure the cameras couldn't see the jokes he was writing. He didn't get why they were so keen to sneak a look. He was trying to fine-tune jokes about the gameshow but as yet, he couldn't really concentrate. The lack of clocks bothered him far more than he thought it would, but he was never the type to get worked up by things. The madness had yet to really begin.

He was then disrupted from his thoughts by the security guards who were ready to take them to the studio. The hour had flown by! Denzel thought he had seen big guys in the National Football League, but these guys made them look as though they were the dweebs he used to push into the girl's bathroom.

The six walked to the studio. Denzel strutted with the confidence of an A-lister about to walk on a red carpet. With his hands in his pockets, his t-shirt untucked and his laces untied, Nate looked like he'd just got out of bed and had gone out for the local paper. Jed was in default smile mode, in a sharp suit, and hair not an inch out of place. That didn't stop him from combing it with his hands, but that was more to show off his expensive bracelet, an anniversary gift from his wife.

Madison looked at both sides of the corridor, the only one of the six to do so. She noticed there were photos of the six of them at various points in their lives. There was no shortage of cute ones, including cherished holiday photos, landmark schooldays and with beloved family members, close friends and adorable pets. Others were less flattering, including ones in courtrooms, police stations and turbulent relationships they would have rather forgotten.

Yasmeen's anger had abated, replaced with a calmer disposition that still flickered with intensity. A sensation not felt by Linda, who walked slower than the others and kept looking back. Suddenly, she began to run away from the entrance to the studio. She didn't get far, and it only took one security guard to handle her.

Denzel looked over at her in surprise and wondered how many security guards would have needed to stop him. Jed and Yasmeen looked impatient.

"We may as well get it over with," said Madison.

"You'll need something more imaginative than that to get out of here" replied Nate with a hearty chuckle. "That would have been on page one of their security handbook." Linda still looked white as a sheet.

With that, the music started, as the host Buck Jackson came down, or Bulletproof Buck as he was known to those who had tried to get him punished for some inappropriate flirting with his female interns. He was the ultimate definition of a man who felt at home on a stage. Five foot 10 and with his signature goatee and trademark wit and energy, he had been the obvious choice to host. Previously a mildly successful TV actor, his career turned with the success of his podcast "What Gets Me…", a colourful weekly rant that had audiences in stitches. When he started stealing scenes in comedic panel shows, a career as a gameshow host was the natural extension. But he had never hosted anything like this.

In a flamboyant purple suit that shimmered in the bright lights, his teeth-filled grin was infectious, even if it was wholly insincere. "Welcome people. Welcome you magnificent, wonderful, fantastic people. I love you all. And because I love you so much, I'm here to present the greatest gameshow ever. Sure, we've seen celebrities out of their comfort zone before. But I'm gonna remind you, the winner gets $7.2 million! Crazy money! But on *Wheel of Phobia*, we're spicing it up. Each time I'm here with you all, I'm going to be spinning that wheel, and one of these six celebrities is going home. But that's not it for them. Not only is the $7.2 million cash prize gone, but they also have to do a planned challenge based on their worst fear. And it's top secret. Heck, I don't even know what the challenges' are gonna be. The question is, which of the six will be chosen to face their fear tonight?"

And with that, he walked each of them on stage and the name of each contestant was read out as they headed to the male and female sections.

Despite being a churchgoer and married man with four teenage children, it wouldn't have surprised anyone who knew him that he went straight for the women and greased up the charm. "Hello ladies, let me say you are all looking lovely this evening. Don't they all look incredible?" and looked out at the audience. "I did not realise we were hosting a fashion show tonight," and he laughed. Linda laughed awkwardly, while Yasmeen's scowl was unchanged. Madison glared back at him, something that didn't go unnoticed by Bulletproof Buck, though the cameramen were experts at hiding any awkward close-ups from viewers at home.

"I have to ask the question that we all want to know. Well two questions if you fine ladies will indulge me. "How nervous are you for tonight? Give me a number!"

"About 1,000," said Linda, completely seriously though everyone laughed. "I'm really scared."

Buck put his arm around her. "Let me tell you this. This show isn't for weak people. And I know you're not weak. You are brave. And you will do this."

Linda smiled but she was still pale and trying not to shake.

"How about you, Yasmeen?"

Yasmeen held up five using her fingers.

"I can see you're not too chatty tonight," laughed Buck. "Ah, don't worry. I can talk enough for us both!"

Anticipating the question, Madison gave a five too.

"I'm not sure about that, you look more nervous than Linda and Yasmeen," said the shiny-suited presenter and laughed loudly before she had the chance to respond. "Okay, which famous figure, dead or alive, would you most want to walk through that door for a pep talk?"

Linda said her ultimate musical hero Whitney Houston and quietly but beautifully began to sing the chorus of "I Wanna Dance with Somebody", which got Buck making some rather smooth moves. "You move just like Tom Hanks did when I sang for him," said Linda, pleased at being able to reference such a pleasant memory and for being able to finish a sentence coherently.

"Where's a massive keyboard so we can play Chopsticks!" joked Buck and comedically gestured as though there might be one nearby. "Now, how about you, Yasmeen? Say I could summon anyone from history to walk through that door, who would you choose?"

There was a silence as Yasmeen awkwardly looked around, as though hoping to find inspiration.

"You're lucky I'm not paid by the minute," said Buck with perfect comedic timing.

"Well, … I guess… Boadicea would be useful. She was a proper badass."

"Oh, she'd kick ass all right!" bellowed Buck. "Which would be very bad news for my suit," as he showed off how shiny it was with various poses. Once the laughter died down, he moved along.

"How about you, Madison?"

"Well, Coco Chanel would be great." She was going to give a lengthy answer about how much her style, ambition and perseverance had influenced and inspired her, but Buck cut her off so in sync that no one would have known.

"Great answer there from Madison," said Buck as he grinned at the multi-millionaire to let her know they were even. "Now, we know everyone is desperate for me to spin that wheel," he said in a loud, infectious voice. "I am, too. You can trust me on that. Before I do, I want to ask you guys two simple questions. Different ones to the ladies, you know me, I'm all about fresh material. I mean, feel this jacket!" And he got all three guys to touch it and didn't let them go until they looked impressed.

"Question time. In one word, describe how you feel right now?"

Denzel thought for a few seconds. "Controlled," he said confidently.

"Expectant," answered Jed in a guarded fashion.

"What, this is a gameshow?" joked Nate. "I thought I was coming to pick up my takeaway!" And he and the host laughed, highlighting the "Sometimes Funny" slogan on Nate's t-shirt, too.

"I will need that word, though," insisted Buck. "Not letting you off that easy."

"Fun," shouted out Nate, and he waved to the crowd, who responded with loud cheers.

"And next question for you three," said Buck, with a long pause for dramatic effect. "If you could have someone with you right now for some comforting words, someone alive and not famous, who would it be?"

"It has to be my mama," answered Denzel without needing to think. "She's been with me every step of the way. Always been my rock, always had my back. I know she's watching right now and shouting at the screen."

Jed pointed to his heart, knowing the added gesture would make it look more sincere. "My wife, Joycelyn. We've been married 21 years. I can't imagine life without her."

Nate smiled and took out a photo from his wallet. "This is Zeus, my adorable Pug. He is the messiest dog ever, and I miss him already. He chews up all my furniture, doesn't use the toilet properly and falls asleep during movies. Pretty much like my last flatmate but far cuter!"

While all three had received a positive response, Zeus certainly won that round.

Following something in his ear, Buck looked up at the screen, which caused the six to look up too. In big letters was the question, "Who will be chosen tonight to do their challenge?" Madison, Yasmeen and Jed instinctively knew that logically, each answer should be around 17%. The three had all been heavily involved with the financial elements of their businesses and had a high level of mathematical knowledge. In fact, Nate was the predicted "winner" with 41.2%. Madison was last with 8.1%. They didn't know if that made them popular or unpopular.

"Could that be what awaits Nate?" said Buck in a loud voice to the crowd. "We won't have to wait long now. Just before I do, I will ask each of the six to pick out a ball from this bag." After each had chosen one, they were then placed in a machine that had several routes to the bottom, with six spaces that blocked a route once it was filled.

It finished as:

Nate Reeder: Purple 1
Linda Mayes: Black 2
Madison Larouch: Red 3
Denzel Harker: Green 4
Yasmeen Kahley: White 5
Jed Dexter: Yellow 6

"As I know you're all aware, one of these six will be knocked out as soon as that wheel finishes. And they will have to carry out something they don't want to do. And they have absolutely no idea what it will be. But we're all desperate to know."

Nate laughed, but the other five were silent.

"Are you ready?" shouted Buck to the crowd to an ecstatic response. "I don't think you are!" His voice resonated even louder, clapping for a bigger impact. The audience was completely enraptured, and the atmosphere was electric. With a final scream, he spun the wheel. It was showtime.

The six were mesmerised. They'd already seen it spin several times before, but watching it with the stakes so high was like watching the car you're in crashing in slow motion whilst being stared at by judgemental strangers. And so they stood, going through all the emotions as the crowd whooped and the lights seemed to get brighter. Finally, though, the wheel was slowing down, even if that only increased the noise.

It was stopping on the yellow slot of Jed Dexter. Typical, he thought. The oldest one out of the way first. His lawyers would find that very interesting.

But as it was grinding to a halt, it just had enough energy to move onto the next slot, covered in black. There was a momentary silence as the crowd processed this dramatic new information, and the cameras captured the contrast in expressions perfectly. Linda's scream as she went from relieved to realising she'd been chosen was glorious and ended up as the most shared gif that night. Jed's calm exterior was impressive, though body language experts were able to point out how much his eyes showed his immense relief.

Linda looked utterly crestfallen and was helped to stand up straight by the remaining five. After waiting for her to compose herself, but realising its futility, Buck went over.

"Oh, Linda," as he gave her a hug. "According to the betting, you were totally safe. Among the safest! This game, I tell you. That's what is gonna make this show so crazy, so legendary, so outrageous. The first of many twists and turns."

The slumped Linda was carried as much as escorted out. The big screens within the studio changed to showing Linda's video, made just before she and the others had entered the studio. The chattering audience all hushed as Linda's nervous smile was conveyed, at odds with her distraught reaction just before leaving.

"So, hey everyone," she smiled in her charming southern accent while blowing the red hair away from her face. "As y'all know, I'm Linda Meyes. Since before I was born, I had music in my blood. My momma was a piano teacher, and my father played the cello. That's how they met and why I'm here. I've been to singing classes since I was out of my stroller. I've been playing the guitar since I was seven. I love music so, so much. Being able to play music for y'all was a dream. Having three top ten albums meant the world to me. Having a cameo in *Lost Sweethearts* and singing the theme tune were things I could never have imagined."

She was made aware of something on the screen and her smile disappeared so fast you'd have struggled to believe it was the same person sat there. "I'm here because I've made mistakes. I cheated on my darling husband even though he was going through cancer radiation treatment. I just felt lonely and sad and neglected. It's the biggest mistake I've made in my life. He's my one true love. 'Dream of My Life' was all about him, and I know I hurt him. I let all my fans down, too."

The 27-year-old started to cry and talk in a more flustered manner. "I know that's not the only reason I've fallen out of favour with you. I take my charity work really seriously. I know what it's like to be poor. After my father lost everything when I was 12, I had to give up all my music classes and fancy school and I know how tough it is. We had to give our dog away as we couldn't afford to keep him. I know what it's like when people treat you different. I had no idea my Red Revelation charity was not giving out money as promised. I swear to you I had no idea. The fact those food centres shut down due to lack of funding broke my heart."

There was another pause as she wiped away tears. "Life hasn't been great the last few years. But I'm on here because I know I can win you back. Once you get to know the real me, you can see that I'm a good person. I'm a kind and genuine person. I just want to share my music with y'all."

While this was being shown, Linda was led away into a car, which was heading to a local airport. No one spoke to her and there was just a long silence. "What happens now? Where am I going?" she asked, more than a little scared. There was no response from anyone, just stony expressions from muscular strangers. She looked unsuccessfully for the camera and then stared into the distance blankly.

One of the security team answered his phone and handed it to Linda.

"Hello Linda, it's Selina," said the voice with forced politeness.

"I'm freaking out," screamed Linda. "You have no idea how afraid I am of heights. I've tried every form of therapy you can think of. People act like it's some natural thing to be up in the air! It isn't! I'm petrified! Don't make me do this!"

"Linda, you have to pull yourself together," replied Selina, almost robotically. "You agreed to face it. You signed the contract. You know there was a strong chance you were going to have to get on a plane. Besides, you've done it before."

"A few times, but I was so doped up on medication I was barely aware of it. And I had all my breathing podcasts on my phone. And I was with family. I can't do this!" And she tried to get out of the car, but security stopped her before she even got to the locked door handle.

"You are facing this challenge. That's the game you signed up for. You'd have accepted the cash prize if you won and you knew you'd have to face the consequences if you didn't," finished Selina with a Siberian coldness. The security guard took his phone back.

Linda knew that was true. But she also knew it was far more than about the money. She had wanted people to see her and understand her and love her again. The reason it hurt even more was because she had been eliminated before people could really get to know her. Linda had planned to play more of her music and let the audience into the stories behind them, making a mockery of those internet rumours she used autotune and could barely play guitar. She'd been desperate to convey all the warmth and knowledge she'd been unable to when she was a judge on a talent show for three weeks before she was abruptly let go.

"You just aren't bonding with the contestants," the producer had told her in a hallway before he fired her. "The people in the studio and at home can't stand you either." Then they hired Melania Rosas, a Latin sensation who had been her best friend. But that was before Linda had been sleeping with her husband. Once Melania discovered it, photos of the affair were leaked to the press. Melania's husband went crawling back, while Linda's husband decided to leave her and file for divorce. Not before a sympathetic TV Interview from a hospital bed where he admitted how betrayed he felt. Which went nicely with the interview done a few days before where Melania's husband revealed his regret at falling for Linda's "persistent charms".

She had failed as a wife, as a mistress, as a guest judge, and as a contestant, she had failed again. And now the worst part of the nightmare was about to begin.

Linda had no idea how long she was in the car before it stopped and they came to what looked like a private airport. There was only a small aeroplane that from its size was clearly used for domestic flights, though from its far from spotless exterior, not too often. Linda had been desperate to leave the car, now she would have given anything to stay inside. She started screaming and found she couldn't stop, eventually being dragged into the plane by security guards who already had earplugs put in. Selina really did think of everything.

As she slowly went up the steps and narrow hallway into the plane, Linda was shocked to find out she wasn't alone. There was only one empty seat at the front. But that wasn't what most caught her attention. Everyone inside was poor. It was clear by how malnourished they were and how beaten down they all looked, even without the rags they were wearing. The random mix of people were mostly asleep or close to it. Those awake made some light jeering sounds, but Linda wasn't sure if they were aimed at her. She didn't trust herself right now, with all her energies being focused on imagining herself anywhere else.

"Where are we going?" Linda asked a friendly-looking girl of about six in the most normal voice she could come up with. "It's a surprise," said the girl smiling, as she continued playing with her faded teddy bear. "You know, it's my first time on a plane. Isn't that amazing?"

Linda tried not to look scared in front of the happy child, but she just couldn't get why anyone would willingly go into a machine which could fail at any moment and fall out of the sky. Or be so happy about it. She wanted to ask more, but the young girl looked so engrossed playing with her tatty teddy bear that it would have taken more energy and concentration to talk with her that Linda just didn't have. She looked over to the girl's mother, who wore a dress that the auburn-haired Southerner couldn't help but notice was faded and torn and had mostly likely been donated.

"Ah, don't mind the others," said the mother, who despite being in her late twenties had the complexion and solemnity of someone who had a tough life. "Don't take it personally. We've just been waiting a while. We were told we couldn't go until the last passenger arrived. You don't mind if I sleep, do you? I'm really tired."

The 27-year-old singer was desperate to know more, but people had started to fall asleep, even the ones who had hissed at her earlier. Linda was exhausted but was far too stressed to sleep. The Memphis native looked away from their faces and tried not to stare at what they were wearing. She knew that feeling of having second-hand clothes and the judgement from strangers, whether they said anything or not. It took her back to being a teenager and that feeling of being less human, less worthy.

"Hello, passengers. I'm sorry our final passenger took so long, but now she has arrived, we will be lifting off momentarily," said the pilot in a voice that resonated with calm and experience. That did wake some of the others up, though not the girl's mother, who had clearly been shattered.

And the petrified Linda gripped onto whatever was strongest to try and keep herself calm. She had naturally pale skin and freckles she had grown to love, but she was white as a sheet, with frenzied eyes that conveyed the terror within her. She tried to remember what the podcasts and her psychologist had said, but her mind struggled to remember anything. And when she looked to the others for support, they just scowled and glanced at their watches. They had clearly been waiting a long time and there was no point trying to obtain their forgiveness.

"You seem nervous," said the young girl and reached out her hand to Linda's. Linda wanted to show how grateful she was, but she didn't want to look up. She had to stay sane. All she wanted to do was scream until it was over, but she knew if she started, she would never stop. Instead, the Southern singer focused on the teddy bear. Despite its poor condition (including a missing ear), it really was very cute and had been lovingly treated.

"You'll be ok," said the girl. "Me and Teddy will look after you."

She wasn't sure how long after, the plane started to go up in the air, causing Linda to grip a bar as though she was hanging onto a ledge with burning lava below. She kept thinking about the highlights of her career. Meeting her husband Louis after he heard her singing "The Memphis Mermaid" in a local talent show and sought her out in person after her performance. Her first record contract by an executive who told her he had the finest voice in his 20 years in the business. Her first gold record. Her two number one albums on the country and western charts. What good times they had been.

At some point within her halcyon daydreams, she felt a tap on the shoulder, causing her to jump, startled. It was the pilot who was smiling at her. He had grey hair within a slightly receding hairline, and wrinkles that dominated his face, but his kind eyes and caring smile were what people would notice most.

Linda was so grateful. She had no idea the man was an actor who specialised in the "sweet grandfather" role and had been typecast as being a good Samaritan throughout most of his career. He also had no idea how to fly a plane. Which didn't matter as it was being controlled by someone off-camera, but the man had practiced enough to look convincing. Everyone on the plane knew who Linda was. They were all actors and knew the role they were playing in this performance.

"I asked you here for a reason, Linda," he said in a soft voice. "I know you're afraid of heights, so I can only imagine how tough this is for you. You're not the first person to have that fear. My own mother has it." That wasn't true, and that wasn't in the rehearsal script, but Frank, or Toby, to give him his real name, did like a little improvisation.

"My mother doesn't," said Linda quickly, as though she had to say it before the world was about to end. "She loves it. Rollercoasters, skyscrapers, hot air balloons, helicopter rides, you name it. She's never said anything, but I know she's disappointed in me. She sees me as a coward who can't share in something that gives her so much pleasure."

"You're not a coward, Linda," said Frank reassuringly. "Everyone is afraid of something. Yours is just very common. But see, we are in the air and everything is fine. I've been flying for 35 years and not had a single problem. Not to mention I have the best co-pilot around."

Linda didn't want to look out of the window with him, so instead looked at the other passengers, who were now all asleep. So calm and peaceful.

"You can't grab onto that bar any harder," reasoned Frank. "Come to the cockpit with me. Trust me, nothing will happen."

And very gingerly, she followed him. As soon as she released her grip, she realised just how hard she had been holding on. The indentations of the bar were all over her hands.

Frank noticed the marks but chose not to say anything, which Linda was grateful for. "You know, I'm actually repaying a favour. My daughter is a fan of yours," added Frank, in an even warmer tone. "Even before she heard your music."

Linda's grin soon changed to bemusement, which brought an even wider grin from Frank.

"It's because my daughter loves horses," said Frank, as he kept an eye on the controls, especially with his co-pilot asleep. "So when she saw your album cover, she bought it before she knew who you were or what you sounded like. She really likes the songs, too. I've listened to them in the car with her on the way to my parents, her grandparents. 'Heartbreak on the horizon' especially.

"I can't go on like this, where tainted triumphs are like a faded kiss," he sang with feeling, if not the correct pitch. "You might just be a better singer than me though," he added, winking.

For the first time in hours, Linda found herself relaxing. And that meant Frank had her right where he wanted her.

"I'm going to let you in on a secret," he said, leaning in closer towards her. "But you can't tell anyone. I know they really wouldn't want me to be telling you this."

Linda nodded and Frank continued in a quieter whisper. "The original plan was for you to jump tonight. But with the winds it would be too dangerous, so instead we changed planes and got some extra passengers whose plans fell through at the last minute, to help cover costs. Instead, we're flying to an exotic island, and from there, another pilot on a different plane will take you to jump at a height of 20,000 feet."

"That's high! Really, really high!" She breathed in heavily. "So, who is everyone else on this flight?"

"I've never met any of them before, but I think they're from some charity that helps reward people who have spent all of their lives looking after loved ones in hospitals or treatment centres. They're pretty destitute from all the medical bills and people who society tends to forget. So this charity, The CareBearers, I think they're called, pays for them to go on some big expensive trip as a treat. They're good people. They even snuck in a young girl who just beat some rare immune disease after spending all her life in the children's ward, and her mother. There was a late cancellation with the plane they were going to go on, so I said they should come on this one and I'd fly them."

"That was nice of you. Kindness is really important in life."

"You know, Linda, I can see you still look nervous," said Frank as he noticed that though Linda's words were coherent, her face was still full of terror. "I want you to relax. Flying is one of the most natural things in the world. Why don't I show you how easy flying is? That way, being so high up tomorrow will seem as normal as brushing your teeth. Let me show you some of the different buttons and what they do.

"So let's start with an easy one. That's the radar. Over here we have the navigation controls, the altitude indicator, the direction finder. Honestly, it's just like driving a fancy car really. Most of these are for show. Just to make us look smarter. Whatever you do, don't ever press this red button while we're in the air. It would cause the plane to cr-"

As already planned, a sudden tilt of the plane meant that Linda lost her balance and fell into the controls. There was an explosion of noise, as a siren went off and all other kinds of chaotic noises and flashing lights. In reality, the button wasn't connected to anything, but Linda had no idea. She thought she had caused a disaster. And that's what they all wanted her to think.

"Oh no, what did you do?" shouted Frank. "You pressed that red button! The one I just told you not to press while we're in the air. Linda, what have you done?!"

The co-pilot Rose (Meryl in the outside world) woke up and quickly realised the situation. "She didn't remove the fuel gauge, did she?" she said, gloriously incredulous. "Oh my God, why would you do that?" She put her hands to her face and then her head and screamed. The officious-looking 41-year-old with her black hair up, outfit impeccably tailored, had been hoping to land the part of the head pilot but had failed. Rather than sulk, she was going to put on the performance of a lifetime.

"We're gonna die! And just two weeks before my sister gets married. I was going to be maid of honour. I even loved the dress they chose. No, it's not fair! Why now?"

The tears hadn't been planned, but they sure looked spectacular. Hearing noises from the passengers, Frank grabbed onto Rose. "Pull yourself together. Those people need us to be leaders. This job is a calling. For good times and bad. And now you will explain the situation as best you can. Just don't say it was Linda that caused this. Say it was technical difficulties. Be sure to explain to get them ready for the parachutes."

"I can do that," said Rose, as she wiped away the last of her tears and regained her composure. She really was good. Opening the door meant the wailing and screaming could be briefly heard over the quiet prayers of the other passengers. Linda was glad that she couldn't hear things much when the door was closed again. She was struggling enough as it was.

The hysterical redhead kept shaking. "I'm so sorry. I don't know what to say. It's all my fault. I-"

"Listen, Linda, you need to be quiet for a moment while I tell you something important." His voice dropped to a whisper. "There's no time," he said in a faint but urgent tone. "This plane is going to crash very soon so I'm going to level with you. There are only two parachutes that work. Yours and mine, one I carry with me whenever I fly anywhere. This wasn't the original plane. It was switched at the last minute because there were problems with the other one. Like I was telling you earlier. This one is usually only for demonstrations and isn't meant for commercial flights. Those parachutes may look real, but they're about as much use as a used handkerchief. We have to go now!"

Linda looked back at Frank's intense glare for some assurance that this was a joke, but Frank kept going in the same vein. "You need to make a decision and fast," he said impatiently. "Everyone on this plane is going to die. I have the get-out-of-jail-free card for you and me. But it has to be used now. Now!"

Linda was white as a sheet and stuttered out a question. "If... by chance anyone does survive, will...they know that we left them with the fak..., less effective parachutes?"

"No," said Frank with a devious smile. "They look exactly the same. They'll never know. But I need to get an answer right now! Are you in?"

Linda nodded. Frank took the top two ones off and began to connect her to one of them. "Here, take the other parachutes to them. We have to act normal until we jump. Do things as we would otherwise do, so they don't suspect anything."

Linda opened the door and handed them over, deliberately avoiding eye contact with the other passengers.

The girl who had earlier been playing with the teddy bear was now quiet, like everyone else on the plane. Linda looked at her but said nothing to her or Rosa, who was helping connect the group's parachutes.

Frank had already set his up and checked Linda's was all set up correctly before facing the passengers. "I know you are only here because you were chosen for the good and kind works you've done for loved ones. Or in one case I think, complete strangers. We may be up in the sky, but you are the real angels. Helping the sick, the poor and the underprivileged. Working with addicts, former convicts. Terminally ill children. This would have been a once-in-a-lifetime chance for you to go to Barbados. Unfortunately, there has been a technical issue. The fuel gauge has been affected by the skarilion chord and the fuel aqua marator isn't strong enough to be fixed. As Rose has explained to you, we will all need to jump very soon. Luckily, we all have parachutes, so you will be fine."

There was some crying and gasps as the actors all displayed a hugely realistic set of reactions.

One of them spoke out. "I just don't understand how that marator thing isn't strong enough..."

"There's no time for questions," said Frank passionately. "It will only get more dangerous the longer we leave it. If we jump now, we're in good terrain, so we have a chance. If we leave it too much longer, we'll end up in the middle of the ocean."

He looked at the group. "As Linda is the most afraid of heights, I'm going to jump just after her, just to make sure she's ok. Rose will check all of yours are done up correctly before you jump."

The little girl went up to Linda and handed her the teddy bear she had been holding. "I know you're scared. You can borrow Teddy." Linda tried to give it back, but the girl insisted. "You can give him back to me when we land."

Her mother started crying but was able to hide her tears from her daughter. "Such a brave little girl. I'm so proud of her. Everything she has gone through and she's still thinking about others."

Linda looked at her parachute and then the girl. The mother and her daughter looked at her, waiting for Linda to say something, but Linda just looked down at her shoes apologetically. "I'll make sure I give him back to you," said Linda quietly after a long silence. Viewers at home later had to rewind and turn the volume up, as she said it in such a whisper.

"It's time!" Frank shouted. "Remember, this is an automatic chord, so you don't have to do anything. Just jump as soon as I open that door, ok?!"

Linda was too petrified to say anything. She wasn't even able to stop her feet from shaking.

"I'm opening this door on five. You'll go first, then me, and Rosa will have the others in order."

"I can do this, I can do this, I can do this," said Linda on repeat, though it just made her seem in a trance. She didn't hear the numbers go down to one.

But she did notice the door opening and the scream she gave when Frank nudged her out of the plane.

Her scream didn't last long. Neither did her jump. A split second after being pushed out of the plane, she realised she had landed on something. Was she dead? How could she be dead? What had she landed on? Why did it feel so soft?

She slowly opened her eyes, petrified as to what horrors she would see, before noticing she was lying on a deep mat, surrounded by bright lights, high walls and lots of video cameras. Finally focusing on the sounds around her, she recognised what the loudness was. It was laughter. Unconfined, uncontrollable, unmistakable laughter. Standing up, she looked at their faces, before she turned around and noticed how they were all pointing at her and laughing.

She was close enough to hear some of the comments. "Oh my God, that was hilarious," howled a guy in his forties to his wife. "She kept going on about her fear of heights and was inches off the ground the whole time!"

"A coward and an idiot," roared an old lady.

"You know, mummy," said a teenage girl to her mother, stifling a laugh. "Linda should be in a Wizard of Oz remake. She needs a heart, courage and a brain."

Looking down at the studio, Selina looked at her notes then smiled. The actors had occasionally gone off script. Already in character, "Frank" had chosen not to use much of the terminology they had gone over in rehearsal, but she couldn't argue with the raw beauty of how it played out. He had assured her that inventing technical terms would make it funnier, and he was right. The crowd had been in stitches. It had gone better than even she had imagined.

Below, Linda turned around to see all the actors taking off their microphones and costumes. "Better than theatre!" screamed Toby, his role now done. "The joy of being live while also reaching a worldwide audience. You can't beat it!"

The little girl went over to Linda. Her cute smile was replaced with a cold, professional one. "I'm down half my paycheck," she muttered bitterly as she slammed the teddy bear she had just picked up back onto the floor. "I bet my dad you would give me the parachute. And your sweaty hands were gross! Like a pig." As she walked off, she swore and kicked out at a table leg.

Linda saw on the big screen there was a question entitled "What will Linda do with her parachute?

"Give it to the little girl" was 61.1%
"Offer it to another passenger" 11.3%
"Tell the passengers Frank's plan" 8.2%
"Keep it for herself" 19.4%

Once the laughter eventually stopped, it was clear who had guessed incorrectly, even without the red lights above their head that vastly outnumbered the green ones. The fact that there had been a bonus cash prize for those guessing correctly meant there was a real mix of elation and disappointment, with added hatred now coming to the fore as the losers looked out onto those collecting their winnings. Those outside using their real money had lost out on even more. More people resented her now than ever before.

As she walked off towards the exit, she realised how alone she felt. She had failed again and this time there was no way back.

II

While all this was happening, each of the five was in the rooms in their own world. Denzel was lying on his bed listening to music, having earlier been cooking and working out in the homemade gym. Nate was working on new material and watching some comedies from the film list, as well as a few comedian-led sitcoms. Madison had been reading a lot. Some were business books, as well as a biography of Yves Saint Laurent. Jed was continuing to write his autobiography and making steady progress. He couldn't think of a title but was fairly confident something would come from his experiences in the show. Yasmeen had been meditating and listening to some spiritual music while drawing and reading up on Asian sculptures. No one had said more than a sentence to each other.

Suddenly, Selina appeared with a smile on her face, which Nate reasoned was the smile you'd have if you stole cash off of a blind orphan.

"Welcome again," she said with a smile viewers would not see due to deliberately chosen camera angles. "The first challenge has been completed. We are working on updating our facilities for the next challenge."

"How did it go?" asked Denzel impatiently.

"What was the challenge?" demanded Jed.

"When is the next one?" wondered Nate.

"Ah, now that would be telling," said Selina with a smirk. "All I am at liberty to reveal is that the challenge is completed and the odds of you winning the jackpot have now improved to 20%. Before I leave, any further requests? This visit is merely a courtesy. From now on, you will need to write what you need on that screen and you will receive a written response shortly after."

"We require a maid!" Jed yelled, exasperated. "Living in the same quarters as this young 'gentleman' is like living with a five-year-old. Honestly, I can't begin to imagine what squalor he grew up in."

"Geez, it's not like the king of England is visiting," said Nate with a shrug.

"His majesty would be appalled," responded Jed with derision. "Have you ever used a napkin or even a plate? I hear both are quite fashionable."

"No maid!" said Selina firmly. "You can't have any contact with the outside world. When your clothes and sheets get dirty, just leave them in the hamper and they will be cleaned."

Not wanting to miss her chance, Madison spoke up with authority. "SOMEONE finished all the cookies without checking with the rest of us. There are none left. There's no need to buy any more. I just need the ingredients to make some myself."

"Hang on, your family owns half the city. Just get some sent over," said Nate, who spoke while still eating, much to the despair of Jed.

"Don't do that," replied Madison assertively, as she wrote the list of ingredients down and handed it to Selina. "These are my own cookies. Even I don't know the family recipe."

"I'd like some coloured pencils, you know, if you have them," requested Yasmeen.

"Hey, wait… Selina! Are you sure we can't get at least one clock here?" demanded Nate as he saw Selina about to walk off. "The others may not mind, but I write my best jokes after the watershed," he added, laughing, though no one else joined in.

"No clocks are allowed," said Selina firmly. "That was previously discussed as non-negotiable. I'll get you the other items requested." And with that, she was gone, and the cameras were now able to move again naturally, having been under strict instruction not to show her.

"No idea if it's light outside or not," muttered Denzel. "Like being in Vegas without all the fun."

"Something tells me Linda wouldn't have liked Vegas," said Nate, with a hint of a smirk.

At Linda's name, the room went eerily quiet. The five looked around at each other, wondering if someone should say something. The truth was they were still really happy to see the back of Linda. All she seemed to focus on was music, and her sad and desperate vibes really did bring down the mood. Denzel, Jed and Yasmeen had no idea who she was, Nate had only heard one of her songs and Madison only recognised her because she had seen *Lost Sweethearts* with a boyfriend.

The uncomfortable truth was that they all knew even if they had liked her, they were still glad she had gone. Every person leaving meant a better chance of winning for those remaining and less chance of having to do that challenge.

The five went off to do their own things and didn't talk again for the rest of the day.

With no clock, people woke up at different times. Madison awoke to see Yasmeen was drawing in the corner of the room, where the natural light was best. The heiress quickly put on a robe and went to get herself a drink before she noticed a piece of paper stuck to the fridge with an arrow pointing right. There were the ingredients for the cookies. "Extra sugar on mine," said the note initialled NR. Below that were further updates. "Less sugar please," signed Maverick. "I'll have some," next to Jed's initials, and "wheat free," accompanied by several exclamation points and then Yasmeen's name.

"How long was I asleep?" wondered Madison as she drank her glass of water. She grinned at the messages and promised to get right to them as soon as she done some gym work and then showered.

She wondered what the guys were doing. They certainly weren't in the living room, though walking towards the guys' room, she did see some lights on and hear some form of activity, even if the door was closed. It sounded like Nate was acting out a comedy routine and Jed was trying to sing opera. Maybe Denzel was asleep. Or else just covering his ears and pretending to be.

A shirtless Denzel sped out of the door and almost knocked her over. "You ok?" he said sheepishly as he went to pick her up. She nodded that she was fine, and they looked at each other with an odd intensity. Realising someone had to break the silence, he went off towards the kitchen. Madison stayed there momentarily, wondering how long Denzel must spend in the gym to get such a toned physique.

Regaining focus, Madison looked in the open door to see that she was right. Nate was trying out different voices for a bit about hecklers, while Jed was singing along to an aria.

"I'll keep it quiet," mimicked Nate, mocking Jed with an exaggerated posh tone, before walking out with his notepad and pen.

"You don't play Renata Tebaldi on low volume," said a beaming and unapologetic Jed.

With only her and Jed in the room together, the different habits of the three were even more stark. Jed was so tidy he could easily have been a butler in a previous life. He'd even filed his books in terms of size and his wardrobe by dark to light. Nate's part of the room looked like he was an unruly five-year-old. Clothes on the floor, food wrappers all over the place, random bits of scrunched-up paper everywhere except in the dustbin. The only thing that had been done with care was some posters of some basketball players she didn't recognise.

Denzel's section was covered with sporting trophies and posters of various different musicians. He had a lot of clothes. He took his fashion seriously. Judging by the order and arrangement of the hangers, he knew what he would wear days in advance. He was a stylish man.

Denzel re-entering the room with a half-eaten croissant and glass of orange juice was the shock she needed to get going. She went back to her room and showered. Once dressed, she entered the bedroom and for the first time, really noticed Linda's absence. Madison was torn between making the most of the extra space and added quiet and feeling guilty about how much she relished it.

Feeling it best not to linger on those thoughts, Madison noticed the coloured sketches that Yasmeen had left on the desk.

"I really think you draw well," said Madison genuinely, as she looked at the impressive detail of various animals. Yasmeen nodded in acknowledgement but clearly didn't want to talk. Closing her book, Yasmeen went into the living room and flicked through different songs on the jukebox, though she couldn't find one she wanted.

Nate was absorbed in the video game he was playing. Having begun with a car-racing game, he'd moved on to Mortal Kombat, his favourite growing up. Enacting the moves, shouting encouragement, and with random moments of chanting "Finish Him," the group had never seen him so passionate. There were all the latest consoles and games, but Nate found himself choosing the classics from his childhood. Streets of Rage, Goldeneye, Mario Kart, Street Fighter and Zelda. Until he knew the latest Knicks' result, he was staying away from the basketball console games.

Denzel was stretching and getting ready for a long workout session. It wasn't the biggest gym by any means, but Selina's crew had done a good job. There was a rowing machine, treadmill, bench press and all the other classics like the horizontal seated leg press, lat pulldown and arm curl machine. He did some stretches and then got ready for his two-hour session.

Jed had finished listening to classical music and was working on his book. At random moments, he would go into the living room with the pretence of grabbing some water or a piece of fruit, but really it was to check if someone was doing something interesting that he could include for added detail.

Madison had some cereal and then began baking the cookies. Happy to feel alone, she got out all the ingredients, noticing with a smile that each came with a flattering description of why the company's product was so good. It was a while since she'd seen the words delicious, scrumptious and succulent in the same sentence. She couldn't help but smile. She'd always hated her family's cookies but could never say anything to anyone, save it got leaked to the press. Baking her own was a way of avoiding all that drama, with the added bonus of reinforcing her own identity.

After a while, Nate had won enough fights as Scorpion and switched the console off. Choosing Chow Mein from the different cuisines, he looked around to see he was the only one in the living room. Since leaving home after dropping out of college, he'd either lived with complete strangers or else lived alone. Being in such close quarters with people he only knew from what he'd read in some headlines was an odd hybrid.

Jed walked in, heading straight for the liquor. Whisky neat, just as he always took it. Jed was a man of tradition when it came to his habits. Always a black coffee to start the day, one glass of juice and three of water during the day, and a shot of whisky most days in the evening, with some milk just before bed. Order was important to him. Chaos was impossible.

He sat down calmly at the dinner table to relax. A calm sip within the madness, reminding him of better times. And just as he brought the glass to his lips, the klaxon sounded. That sound of the devil, of hell and all its evil and insanity. An hour until the next round. He decided there was nothing to be done but to enjoy the glass calmly.

Behind him, the other four had heard the klaxon. It was impossible not to. It was loud enough to wake the dead, or at least anyone with a bad hangover, Nate reasoned.

With Linda gone, Yasmeen was calmer, but Madison still knew not to provoke her. Yasmeen decided to do some quick Pilates exercises before some meditation. She had calmed the mind last time but not relaxed the body. Denzel got out his adrenalin at the batting cage again, Nate had a beer and Madison mostly stared at the wall, wondering what to do.

After an hour sharp, Selina arrived with her usual security team. The five soon got ready and walked towards the studio. Yasmeen looked indifferent, Denzel was focused, while Madison and Yasmeen wore forced smiles. Nate was acting like they were going out for ice cream.

"You need to embrace the crazy!" he told the others. "Either we're closer to getting to the jackpot or we're back to reality and home."

"Yeah, via hell!" said Yasmeen.

Selina's face gave nothing away, but inwardly she appreciated the brevity and pithiness of the remark.

The wheel loomed just as bright, dangerous and ostentatious as ever. For a split second, Madison wondered if the wheel had actually gotten bigger. Like the others, she noticed there were only five names running along the studio lights. Linda had been close to the edge even before she was chosen. Whatever happened tonight, Madison promised herself she wouldn't lose her cool.

The five were randomly next to each other, with the male and female sections now removed. Perhaps not coincidentally, that gave Buck more space to work with.

"Welcome back, you glorious people!" shouted Buck as he ran into the frenetic crowd as though he were running for president. The truth was, they would have given him their vote without him needing to ask. "It's time for another round of *Wheel of Phobia*," he shouted to his adoring fans. "Are you ready?!"

They really were in the palm of his hand. He was part comedian, part preacher. He owned the stage, and he sure controlled the people watching. "I ain't moving until I know you're ready." And the noise was once again ramped up.

"Now that's more like it," he said and bounced down the steps to meet the contestants. He wore a bright green suit, with an orange tie. Being the showman he was, he'd checked no one else was wearing any shade of green before going on stage.

"Well," he said to Yasmeen. "There's only five of you left. Tell me what's it like being where you are now?"

"It's like walking in the dark and not knowing where you're going," said Yasmeen, much calmer than her appearance the week before. She wondered why she was chosen first, until she realised she was the one nearest to him.

"Very poetic there," said Buck with genuine sincerity. "I prefer it when things rhyme, but that was nice. I like it."

Buck moved along to Jed, who had mastered the phoney smile.

"Jed, you've been a bit of a mystery to us," said Buck, speaking slower and with added emphasis. "People see you as a dark horse. You're the oldest one here, you've been keeping to yourself more than the others have. So, J-Dog, is this a strategy?"

"Ah, you know me, Buck, er B-Dog, I'm just cool under pressure," said Jed, trying to look as modest as possible. "I'm older than the others, but I've seen more. I've experienced more. I'm ready for this like every other challenge in my career!"

"I like it, I like it!" shouted Buck, as he grabbed Jed's arm in support.

"Madison, sales of the business books and the biographies you've been reading have gone up. Very impressive numbers, very impressive. You're a genuine reader. I just used to pretend to read fancy books. My mamma was so impressed with my fake knowledge she kept buying me more." And his infectious laugh got everyone with him, except for Madison, who had finished the two books she'd started and would have liked the chance to talk about them. But when Buck was on stage, he was the king.

"Nate the Great," said Buck, as he thumped Nate's chest, above a t-shirt that said, 'Genius when sober'. "That's what your fans are calling you. Tell me, what's it like being a comedian in a situation like this?"

"Well not ideal. Linda left before I finished writing her jokes," said Nate, happy that people were laughing even before the punchline. "I mean, usually, people leave after they've heard the jokes, not before," delivered Nate, with perfect comic timing.

It didn't take much to make Buck laugh, but he sure did have an infectious one. "I've been there!" He tried to compose himself, but to the delight of the audience, struggled to keep a straight face. "In my early days, I once had a set interrupted by someone shouting out for more ketchup."

"And did they get it?" asked Nate.

"Nah, the place only had mustard," said Buck, who barely finished the sentence before the place erupted. Buck composed himself before moving on to the final contestant.

"My man, Denzel. I shouldn't stand next to you, or people might look at our physiques and make you feel inadequate," grinned Buck. "You are ripped! Does being in great shape help you deal with this situation?"

"Working out and playing sports does help relax me, yeah. I owe everything to sports. I found book stuff hard, but on the field, it all makes sense."

"Well, we should release a fitness book between us. You can be the Before Guy and I can be the After Guy," said Buck as he grabbed Denzel by the shoulder as though they were posing for a photo.

"But it's now time to check the voting," said Buck in a more professional manner, after hearing something in his earpiece. With that, everyone looked up to the big screen. Madison was top with 34.6%, closely followed by Jed with 32.4%. Nate had 17.3%, Yasmeen had 9.3% and Denzel was last with 6.4%.

"An 8% voter increase since last time!" said the presenter in a loud and impatient voice. "Well done, people! You were badly wrong last time around, let's see if it's any different this time." He looked to the five. "Just like our last episode, you each pick a ball and then drop it into the box."

There was a silence as the five chose the balls and then placed them in a container, where they were randomly assigned a colour.

Madison Larouch: Red 1
Jed Dexter: Purple 3
Denzel Harker: White 4
Nate Reeder: Green 5
Yasmeen Kahley: Yellow 6

"Let's do this!" roared Buck as he started spinning the wheel. The audience was spellbound as they waited to see who this episode's loser was.

If it was easier for the contestants having been through this once before, they didn't show it. The only one who looked remotely at ease was Nate, who stared at the baying crowd with mild amusement.

After swirling round and round, the wheel was getting slower and slower. The cameras focused on Yasmeen, who was drumming her fingers nervously, and Denzel, who was puffing his cheeks out and straightening his posture at regular intervals. But it didn't land on them. Instead, it landed on Jed.

He stared at the wheel intensely, almost as if he could make it move one place if he wished it hard enough. But it just stayed there motionless. The father of two could barely move as he realised what he was going to miss out on.

Farewell to the fame, farewell to the money, farewell to the chance to add more material to his book.

And then his mind started focusing on the upcoming challenge. If they had indeed found out his phobia, he was in big trouble.

Buck was talking and asking him questions, but his mind was too frozen to make much sense. The pretence was blown. Buck gave up after three questions, especially when Jed wasn't even able to nod and it looked like he might collapse. He was helped out of the studio by the security guards and wouldn't have heard the video being shown.

"Hi, I'm Jed Dexter. What can I say? I never thought I'd be on a show like this one. It's not like I even like being on TV. It's different from anything I've ever done before, or what anyone has done before. But hey, I've faced all kinds of challenges in my career, and I will face this one. Sure, the money is nice, and it's nice to think about the number of people I could help with such a significant amount. I've never been afraid of anything in my life, so bring it on."

The last line wasn't the only lie those close to him knew he had told. His love of the camera was well known, and Jed wasn't exactly known for his sincere generosity, either. But it was still a shock to see the difference between the suave, slick and sprightly 52-year-old and the guy who could barely stand up or speak a functioning sentence.

Jed's video continued. "I'm here because I've made mistakes. I'm honest enough to admit I've made them. We've all sinned, but I know I'm in the public eye and was in office, and that means I'm going to be judged harsher than others. I understand, and let me tell you that being your senator was an absolute honour and a privilege. I let you down when I cheated on my wife with the nanny. I still believe in the 'Family Matters' campaign that I was so successful with. I got so many votes, so many, many votes, because you believed in me. You didn't see me just as a silver fox with impeccable manners, you saw me as someone who would fight for you. I know I accepted donations from various disagreeable people who I know my voters weren't fans of, and I campaigned against things they were accused of. But it was only accused. But to think I deliberately sabotaged bills in favour of bribes was completely untrue. I was merely being hypothetical when I was talking with those underhand journalists. Sure, I could have made my language clearer, but it was obvious I was just giving examples highlighting flaws in the process. And I will come back and clear my name."

"Right now, he couldn't even say his own name," zinged Buck to the studio audience once the video finished. "You were closer this time, people, but you were wrong again. And that's why this is the best show in town. We push people to the limit, whether they want to reach it or not. Here at *Wheel of Phobia*, you win big, or you lose big. And tonight, the loser was Jed Dexter. That's it for tonight, but stay alert for updates about Jed's challenge. We know you can't wait!"

As this was going on, Jed had yet to calm down and had started sweating and breathing heavily. It was all the classic symptoms of a panic attack, and he knew how helpless he was in the backseat of a car surrounded by the biggest security guards he'd ever seen in his life. It was just as well he wasn't thinking of the camera capturing his every move, or he'd have been in an even worse state. His suffering was now being enjoyed, or at least watched by, an ever-growing audience on every type of technological device. From being so calm on the exterior, Jed was showing signs of freaking out and people were loving it. They were even guessing what was next. Suggestions included wetting his pants, begging for death, swearing loudly or trying to bribe his way out.

He did none of them, but he was far from in control. The truth was, he wasn't even sure how he could be, when he didn't even know why he was petrified of clowns. He'd obviously repressed something, and no number of psychiatrists had been able to get to the root of it.

The thing was, Jed knew he was a smart man. He'd proven it countless times over the years. Through his "mistake" of giving his rival the wrong interview details for the exclusive internship he was chosen for. Through the illegals he had helped a friend hire for his restaurant before ratting them out just before they were about to be paid. Through his carefully judged gossip at numerous party events when he sensed an underling was trying to get too powerful. And though his brilliant choice of wife. Yes, she was dull as paint and not as attractive as the female interns he regularly hired, but she sure was worth a lot of votes.

And he was even smart with his choice of phobia. Not for him one of the regular ones, where it could be discovered easily. He hadn't known what Linda's phobia was, or any of the others. But a fear of clowns wasn't that popular. I mean, how many people knew what coulrophobia was? He had kept his hidden. He never mentioned circuses or even anything that gave off that connotation. No talk of an elephant in the room, or people being clowns, or references to the circus leaving town or having to clean up after it. And it wasn't like you'd be expected to meet a clown at your regular office meeting. Not a literal one anyhow. Jed even avoided being anywhere near a kid's birthday party too. Jed told himself the idea of a grown adult dressing like a tomato with stupid trousers and shoes was nonsense anyhow. And yet he was still terrified that the producers knew.

That thought was on his mind when the car finally pulled up. He had no idea where it was, but it was remote. It looked like an old theme park, long abandoned like in a spinoff of *The Shining*. It was dark, it was scary and he was desperate to leave. But he wasn't in control. He was taken to a small hut and left there for what was probably a few minutes but felt like hours. Even if he was able to get past the burly security guards, he wasn't sure he wanted to. He had no idea what was lurking in the shadows. And though he considered himself a brave man, he didn't feel like one now.

Suddenly, Selina's formal voice could be heard coming from the loudspeakers that Jed hadn't previously noticed. "Hello, Jed. As you know, you were chosen, and now you must carry out the selected activity. It will be tonight. Think of it like a band-aid. The sooner you start, the sooner it will all be over."

Jed knew that was true, but he also knew he wasn't ready.

Selina's voice continued. "As you'll have gathered, this former theme park is pretty remote. Which makes it perfect for your challenge."

"So, you know what the phobia is?" said Jed quietly.

"Ah, Jed, we know you better than you know yourself. Yours was the toughest to discover; you did have it exceedingly well hidden. In front of you, you will see a screen with a set of instructions. Be sure to read it carefully." And with that, back to silence, even though Jed had the horrible feeling that he wasn't alone.

The 52-year-old, who told people he was 47, slowly walked towards the screen. In big letters was the challenge's title. "Attack of the Clowns."

The cheeky reference to the Star Wars film was completely lost on him but gathered an admiring chuckle from most viewers.

He read it fast at first, and then slower the second and third times as he began to process what it entailed.

Dear Jed. Outside of this tent, you will be led to a maze. In the centre of this maze is the brown door to the exit and the successful completion of the challenge. There are nine other exits, each of which will be guarded by a clown holding a bat. Each clown will have their own colour baseball bat and individual outfit. For the first hour, they will be under instruction not to attack you. After an hour, that instruction will cease and from that point on, clowns will be released at five-minute intervals. We fully recommend you find the exit within the first hour.

Added notes:

- *At ten-minute intervals, the time remaining will be announced. An additional reminder will be announced with five minutes to go.*
- *Each baseball bat that a clown uses can only be used back on that same clown. Failure to follow this task instruction will result in an additional clown being let out earlier.*
- *Clowns are not allowed to run after the hour mark, only to walk. This will be ensured by their feet still being chained.*
- *Even if one of the other nine exits is unguarded or you are able to get past a clown, that exit door will not open. The brown exit door must be located to leave the maze.*
- *At the hour mark, the centre door will remain brown, while the others will all change to multicoloured stripes.*
- *The challenge only ends when you reach the correct exit and leave the maze.*

Jed wondered if the previous challenge had been as bad as this. Nine clowns! He had seen one on his way to work three months ago and had to go straight home. He couldn't eat for the rest of the day, and it took him a week to get back to his regular sleeping pattern. And that was when it was it was broad daylight, and the clown was wearing a suit and carrying a suitcase.

He looked up to see a large clock ticking down from five minutes. So, Jed had a short time to compose himself. He hadn't been the best husband, but he'd been a good father to his two boys. He attended all the big moments and had given advice when they'd asked him. It was more than he'd had from his old man. And sure, Jed regularly cheated on his wife, but she knew it was a marriage of convenience when they first got together. He needed someone from the right background to fast-track him into the political world, and she needed someone sociable and confident to take her away from her domineering father. He could have been more discrete, but she could have been more loving. He wondered what she was thinking, watching him now. A lot of worry, he hoped. It was important he put on a good front for her and his kids. Image was everything in politics.

Jed watched the clock go down to zero, and he jumped up, ready for action. He had an hour; he was going to make it work. Though it was pitch black outside, the maze was brightly lit, far too bright. But he wasn't going to waste time on that.

He soon realised there were going to be no clues. This was purely going to be a memory test. Maybe that was easier, he reasoned. And fitting. He decided the best thing was just to be decisive. It will all look the same, so just keep a fast pace and with some effort and random luck, he would get there.

Viewers watching were impressed by Jed's sudden change in attitude. A man who looked like he'd be knocked down by a feather an hour ago now looked as though he could take on the world.

And so, Jed decided to do a mix of left and right. The exit was most likely in the centre, so just going left or just going right would be a bad idea. Better instead to do a combination of both. Smart, smart, smart. His sons would see him as clever enough to figure out an effective system and brave enough to face his demons. As would all the voters, including the wealthy ones who backed campaigns.

After making a few sprints in different directions he saw his first clown. The explosion of red, with the excessive face make-up, frizzy hair, large nose, striped costume and oversized shoes. And that sinister smile. It was so creepy that Jed just wanted to run. Even if that were within the rules, the former Senator knew it was out of the question. He was struggling even to stand up.

Jed slumped to the floor, feeling like he'd been punched in the gut. He stumbled, trying to get back up, trying not to look at the chained-up freakshow in front of him.

The clown leaned towards him while also waving his red bat and smiling manically. "I'm waiting for you," he said, glaring at him with his crazy eyes before winking.

Jed couldn't stumble out of there fast enough and had to sit down momentarily. He had no idea how long he sat there, but a klaxon and an announcement that ten minutes had passed soon swept him back to his reality.

He thought again of his wife and kids and found the strength to keep going. He still had 50 minutes. Now, he would vary it a bit. A few more lefts amid the rights. He had no idea how many; all his focus was on getting to the next exit. He ran as fast as he could and saw a door as he turned into a corner and saw another clown.

This one was larger and taller than the other. He wasn't in red, but blue. The clown had been sat down and as he stood up, twirling his bat, it was clear he was at least 6'4 and around 16 stone. This time, Jed recoiled like he had been slapped in the face. The clown was enjoying it. He laughed and blew him a kiss. He waited until Jed left before sitting down again.

Jed only just got out of the line of sight before his legs went, and he fell to the floor. He was sick in one of the hedges and unbuttoned his sweaty shirt, something he should have done earlier.

That was about the only clear thought he had. His mind was going out of control as he struggled to process everything as time went on. And yet he found himself unable to get up or move, as time drifted on. Another klaxon and a further ten minutes gone. It couldn't be!

"Okay Jed, you've seen two exits in 20 minutes," he said to himself out loud. "You're going to have to set a faster pace and not get so affected by the freak shows."

Which was true. Unfortunately, he could not keep the same pace as before, and more than once he ran into a clown he had seen earlier. He found it helped not to look at their faces. Sometimes, their expressions were calm. Others, their smile was so bitter and twisted. He avoided looking up and instead focused on the colours. The fact that their baseball bats matched their suit colour was helpful, if more terrifying.

In this period, two klaxons had gone off. Where had all the time gone?

Jed did some quick calculations in his head. He had seen clowns dressed in red, white, black, green, purple, pink, yellow, grey and brown. That was nine, though really, he'd seen some more than once, including that purple-dressed clown at least four times. Hadn't the instruction book said there were ten? That just meant he only had to find one more. And his shoes were not suitable for running. Which gave him an idea. One he should have thought of a while ago.

What if he put something at the beginning of each entrance? Finding a new burst of energy, he sped around the maze as though his life depended on it. Maybe it did? He didn't care which door now. He just knew he could improve his chances. Seeing that purple clown again (What was it with that purple clown?), he took off one of his shoes and put it at the entrance but far enough away that the clown couldn't touch it. That rattling of the chain stayed with Jed even after he had run off.

As he once again met the different clowns, he found avoiding the eyes easier as he looked at the colour of the bats. Having taken off both shoes, both socks and his recovered shirt, he knew five had been done. He'd also been smart enough to remove the laces, so that meant seven. He had been counting when he'd heard another klaxon. The Chicagoan decided from now on, he was going to ignore them, as it would only make him panic.

He could be quicker, but he kept forgetting which routes he had taken and spotting the clothing items he had placed earlier. He found a place where he hadn't placed anything. Could this be it? Jed ran faster. This had to be it, he told himself. It wasn't. Instead, it was the silver-coloured clown from earlier, who had hidden from view for maximum impact. "SURPRISE!"

From thinking he had escaped his misery to this. He staggered out, wobbling as though he had taken a punch from Nate Tyson. The klaxon sounded, with a message impossible to ignore. "You have five minutes left. After that, the first clown will be released."

Jed wasn't sure if the sounds of chains rattling were real or in his head. Wishing for the first time he was large enough for a belt, he took off his trousers, leaving him in just his white underpants. How many doors were left? Was it eight or nine he had seen?

He couldn't wait to find out. He sped round again, manically. He saw buttons and shoes and laces. Maybe there was no unmanned door. Maybe this was all a trick. He wanted to shout and scream and swear, but he knew that wouldn't play well with voters. When he got out of this challenge, if he got out of this challenge, he didn't want anything to embarrass him. His rivals would instead salute his bravery.

And that was all good, until the final klaxon sounded. Maybe that was the challenge? Survive the hour and the rest was all bluster. He had given everything.

But a familiar voice came out on the loudspeaker, and Jed's heart sank.

"The challenger has failed to complete the challenge within the first hour," said Selina's ominously clinical voice. "We therefore move to the next part of the challenge. Starting from now, clowns will be released at five-minute intervals."

And maniacal, sinister laughter. And chanting. "Too late for you; we're coming for you." Over and over. Jed wanted to cover his ears, but he knew that would only slow him down. And he had the chilling thought that he would need his hands to defend himself. Jed was torn about which direction to run in, while also not able to shake the question of which clown it would be.

He didn't have to wait long. He looked up to see a clown walking towards him, feet shackled together but still walking at a sinister pace. He'd been chosen over the other eight in the maze by a viewer who had won the online bid to decide which clown to choose and what to name him. Jed's torture at seeing Chainsaw the Clown, or the purple clown as he knew him, became a viral sensation.

Why did it have to be him? screamed Jed internally. That purple bat tapping against his hands. And that laugh was just toxic, so much evil within just a short sound. The purple monstrosity was walking slowly towards him with a grin that told Jed it was all over.

As with the previous challenges, there were two additional audio packages for viewers. One focused on the psychology of the torture, and one purely focused on jokes. The latter had been far more popular this time around, helped by the "Hot/Cold game". So much so that "Warm, warmer, hot, less hot, cold, freezing, you idiot" became a slogan after the host's game, and the "Freezing, you idiot" t-shirt was the best-selling merchandise that night.

Which would be no consolation to Jed as he was running from the clown. Barefoot and down to his underpants, he used his last remaining bit of energy to sprint away from the demented demon. Jed didn't even know which direction he was going in. He didn't know if he was going left, right or forward, he just knew he had to get away. He hadn't had time to process the thought that he might end up running into another clown. Jed wasn't even looking back. All he could hear was that voice.

Jed kept running and through exhaustion and panic, lost his balance and fell into the hedge. But that wasn't a bad thing. He hadn't noticed before but there was another route. How had he missed it? Focusing harder through a gap in the hedge, he could see a brown door. Unguarded. Could it be real, or was it his fervid imagination? Jed wasn't sure how he could have missed it.

He looked back to see the purple clown coming closer, his teeth grinding as he snarled "I'm here, Jed." Like with the other clowns, he had something distinctive printed on his outfit. In this case, it was "Frankalini's", the name of the 1930s speakeasy that had relied on cheap, and ultimately, unpaid, labour run by a close friend of his.

The shirtless and barefoot Jed had never run so fast in his life. He barged into the door, looking for a key, or a lock or a handle, but instead, he fell through the door as it turned anticlockwise.

He had no idea where he was, but suddenly the chanting stopped, and the bright lights were gone. He opened his eyes to see that he was in a studio. In big, shiny, electric letters he saw the finest words he had ever seen in his life. "Challenge completed."

"You can now go home," said Selina, who seemed to come out of nowhere. "You can pick up your phone, suitcase and other belongings by going to room 120 on the left." Jed looked to see if there was a smile, but there was no flicker of emotion. Instead, he looked at the board and saw that they had been voting on him.

How long will Jed take to complete the maze?

Within 15 minutes: 13.2%
16 – 30 minutes: 6.4%
31 – 45 minutes: 19.4%
46 – 60 minutes: 32.3%
Requires extra time: 20.8%
Fails completely: 17.9%

Jed couldn't concentrate on the numbers, or why some people in the audience had green and red lights above their head. But as he got his breath back, he started focusing on the facial expressions of the people who were staring at him intently. They had been looking at him from makeshift seats made up in a temporary stand all around the maze. Some were laughing, others looked sympathetic, while a few looked away in disgust. What they all had in common was that they were covering their noses. Following their gaze, he looked down at his now-brown underpants. The humiliation was complete.

III

At the house, things were quiet. While the group hadn't gotten to know Jed much more than Linda, his exit felt different. While Jed was the most conniving and insincere, his removal had startled the group for different reasons.

For one, he was older, a fact he seemed both proud of and embarrassed by. He had teenage children, who he was showing photos of at various times, though the more cynical within the group felt that was just to curry favour with viewers at home. They had seen Linda blabbing about her fear of heights in interviews going back years, whereas no one knew what Jed's was, which made it seem worse. The fact that Jed had acted so composed throughout but collapsed like a deck of cards as soon as his name came up brought up uncomfortable questions for the group. If Jed could fall to pieces like that, how would they cope?

Nate was erratically driving on a racing game on the video console, Denzel was burning off restless energy in the gym, Yasmeen was reading about the history of African art and Madison finally had the chance to put the cookies in the oven. Madison was usually relaxed when she baked, but this time, she was restless. She was double-checking the ingredients when she usually knew them by heart. The ten minutes she waited by the oven felt like an eternity.

When the timer went, she carefully took them out and onto the work surface. She was about to announce to the group to come over, but as she was turning around, she saw Nate waiting with a plate and a cheeky smile. He grabbed one of the cookies and seemed shocked it was hot.

Denzel went for napkins and plates, while Yasmeen took the vegan milk out and poured herself a glass. She checked to see if anyone wanted any, but not long enough for them to respond in time before she put it back.

The four sat at the table awkwardly as they each ate their own labelled cookies. Soon, only Jed's remained untouched.

"So, what do we do about Je…" began Madison but looked up to see Nate eating them. "I like to eat," said Nate defiantly. "Besides, not like Jed was going to have them."

The mention of Jed's name caused silence.

"Be honest, did anyone like him?" said Nate without any hint of sadness.

The other three looked at each other but didn't answer.

"Fine, I'll answer it," continued Nate impatiently. "I found him smug and annoying. It was like living next to a museum. "Don't touch that", "Don't you know how valuable this is?", "Do you even know how to use a dustbin?" mimicked the 31-year-old in an exasperated tone.

Denzel reflected on being caught in the middle so many times in his athletic days. Madison smiled as she imagined the pristine Jed and dishevelled Nate repeatedly colliding. Yasmeen wanted to leave but was still hungry.

Madison went to the oven and took out another tray. "I was going to have these tomorrow, but we're all here and they're still warm, so we may as well have them now."

"These are even better than the last batch, cookie girl," said Denzel after he had tried the first one, even before putting some on his plate. It was a sentiment shared by the others.

"So, how do you think old boy Jed did?" asked Nate, before he had finished chewing. "Are we gonna guess what his phobia was?"

"We're probably the only ones who don't know," speculated Madison. "He keeps his cards close to his chest, so everyone close to him is probably finding out for the first time, too."

"I bet it's a weird one," reasoned Yasmeen as she playfully flicked her hair. "He's obviously ashamed of it."

"Or maybe he's just in complete denial," argued Madison. "He figures if he doesn't admit it, it won't seem as bad."

"Not a great strategy in this show," said Denzel suddenly. The mention of the programme caught the others off guard, especially as he hadn't appeared to be listening. But Denzel hadn't finished. "I reckon he'll be ok. He's a smart dude. There's a lot of showbiz to him, but nah, I reckon his smarts are worth a lot right now."

The others pondered what he was saying. Nate wasn't sure he agreed. Here, like in life, humour was important. It was the thing he was best at, and probably the only reason he'd had any kind of dating life. He certainly wasn't muscular or good at sports like Denzel or with that poise or air of intelligence that Jed had. Yasmeen wondered why quiet people were always assumed to be smart, when in her experience it just meant they were boring. Madison kept thinking if he was so smart, how was it that he ended up on this show?

They soon finished eating. Madison had been happy to bake but was grinning for the first time since she had been in the waiting room. Nate switched the video game to *Streets of Rage*, Denzel listened to music on his personal headphones, while Yasmeen started repeating Spanish phrases as part of her language course. Madison just sat on her bed while she tried to make sense of it all. She was too confused to write anything in her diary.

And then there were four.

The next morning, or rather, when they all woke up, as they had no idea if it was daylight or night, there was an air of quiet reflection. The talk at the dinner table was the first time everyone who was in the competition had spoken at the same time, and that had thawed the ice somewhat.

When Nate woke up, he noticed the room was cleaner. Denzel had decided to use some of his energy to clean up the floor. Yasmeen also noticed that Madison had left a book on the table next to hers, as she knew Yasmeen had been asking a lot of questions about it.

When Nate went into the kitchen, he noticed that Denzel was cooking a lasagna. And he was singing to himself. Completely out of tune, but that didn't seem to bother him. Hearing Nate, Denzel turned around and smiled. "Hey, if we're in this entertainment hell, then we sure are gonna eat like kings! Try this, brother. And tell me you ain't had nothing sweeter?"

Denzel handed Nate a spoon with a spicy sauce, and even though spicy food was the last thing he wanted at that moment, he was blown away by just how good it tasted.

"Sweeter than sweet, right?" Denzel said, laughing, and gave him a hug. "Don't worry, my man, I made plenty. I've been up hours. Lasagna will be ready later." And with that, he carried on singing and started chopping up the tomatoes.

With a newfound energy, Nate decided not to play video games but instead went back to the bedroom and wrote jokes. He did his best material in the evening (and usually after a few beers), but without knowing what time it was, he figured the usual rules didn't exactly apply. After a short pause, he soon found himself in a groove, helped by the chocolate bars he kept by his bed.

Even with her Pilates, meditation, scented candles and relaxing music, Yasmeen had found it hardest of all to get a good night's sleep since she arrived. For the first time, she slept soundly, even if she dreamt that it was just her in the show and her name was on every slot on the wheel. She'd woken up sweating, but after changing her outfit and throwing some water on her face, soon went back to sleep. Waking up, the Pilates instructor and vegan influencer smelt the delicious lasagna, did some light stretches, showered and then got back to her Spanish. The 29-year-old had trouble with the difference between "ser" and "estar" but was making progress.

Madison slept the longest of all. She awoke with a new energy and began to write something in her diary. Feeling guilty about why her mind was clearer now, Madison knew it was because there were fewer distractions, and by that she meant people. She thought about watching a film but instead decided to get back to her business books.

A while later, Denzel clinked a glass and shouted out all three names. "I ain't gonna eat this all myself, people." And whether it was his commanding voice or how delicious the lasagna smelt, the three were immediately right at the table.

"You did a great job yesterday with the cookies, Madison, but I'm telling you, I'm the best chef here." And he laughed in an accessible way.

"And if we don't like it?" asked Nate mischievously as he put the food on the plate and added some sauce.

"Then that just leaves more for me," said Denzel, and everyone laughed. "Actually, yeah, I wasn't sure if Yasmeen would be ok with the ingredients, so I checked with the production team and got some vegan options. I didn't want you to miss out."

Yasmeen was impressed. Even with seven years of blogging and making videos on the benefits of veganism, most people she had met were bemused, thinking giving up meat was like going without sleep or sex. She had always cared about animals and had been a vegan since she was a teenager, but the Pilates and meditation came a few years later. People who accused her of following a trend had no idea how much she relied on both. Pilates and meditation gave her such a sense of calm. She knew she couldn't have survived the show without it, especially with her previous experiences of when the public had turned on her.

There was little talk until they finished eating. Though he had extra of the lasagna, Nate still had space for dessert. Checking with the others first, he then had some ice cream, which the others used as an excuse to stay at the table.

"I have to ask," said Madison. "What do you guys think of Buck? Notice anything odd about him?"

"Nah, he's hilarious," said Nate. "He's a great comic actor and his podcasts are really funny. I was going to be a guest on his show at one point, before… well, one thing and another."

"He has a lot of positive energy," said Yasmeen after thinking about it for several seconds. "Too many jokes, though. It's exhausting."

"No such thing as too many jokes," insisted Nate.

"Fun guy, shame he's not into sports," grinned Denzel. "He sure knows how to get that crowd going. I could imagine him as an announcer at Lincoln Financial Field… where The Eagles play," he added, noticing some puzzled looks. "Before I played for the Giants, I used to watch them as a kid."

Madison said nothing as everyone noticed that Nate had eaten his ice cream so distractedly that he had a little around his face. Without thinking about it, Madison wiped it away with a napkin, which surprised everyone. Denzel had a reaction that was different to the others but went unnoticed by the group.

"I'm a bit of a neat freak, sorry," said Madison, embarrassed.

"Don't mention it," said Nate. "Most action I've had in a month." He and Denzel laughed, and Yasmeen even cracked a smile. Madison was mortified.

They decided to watch a film together, and after various playful debates, decided to watch *Mean Girls* and then *Die Hard*. Nate had been making jokes throughout, but knowing both films well, he timed them so it added to the dialogue rather than overstepping it.

At times like this, it was easy to forget how they had felt when they had been sat in that waiting room or how distant they had been when Linda was removed. Even Jed's removal seemed a lifetime ago. Nate had made some sharp observations, which he knew would kill in his next routine. He had always been funny and now felt that if he could get people to forget all that stuff from the past and get them just to focus on his current comedy, he was good. He was really in a writing groove.

Madison hadn't always had a diary. She only really used one in times of great stress. When things had gotten really bad and she first became reviled, it was one of the few things that kept her sane. Despite the risk of it being stolen, she never hid her feelings. And spending time with the other three only confirmed she was glad that Linda and Jed had been the first two to lose. Which only led to an uncomfortable question. If she could choose, who would she next select to leave?

Denzel was thinking along the same lines. He hadn't clicked with either contestant who had left. His coach would have called them wallpaper, dummies or sponges. Wallpaper because you don't notice them, dummies because they lack backbone and sponges because they can't be found when you need them.

He hadn't always clicked with every manager. There were some who just saw his pace, power and strength, but others would listen to feedback and include him in more meetings with the quarterback. And he definitely hadn't gelled with every teammate. It wasn't about being best buds. That's what coach Fuller had said when one of his best friends had been traded after an underwhelming previous season. "Guys like that will drag you down. Forget the sponges and remember, it's all about giving yourself the best chance of getting that trophy," his mentor had told him. And that Super Bowl win together only cemented things. Denzel didn't even take off his Super Bowl ring when he showered.

Going to her room to put on a cardigan, Yasmeen looked at herself in the mirror. Sometimes she thought she was gorgeous, other times hideous. One of the things people forgot about when slagging off influencers as getting rich for no effort was just how personal the abuse got. Though her looks were regularly praised, there was always criticism about her hair, her nose, her jawline, her body shape and whatever else the anonymous trolls could think of. And when she dated a high-profile pop rocker from Future Black, it was even worse. Especially as she had been three years older than the 19-year-old teen heartthrob. The fact the excess insults stopped when he cheated on her by sleeping with a groupie was scant consolation.

The good vibes continued the next day. Denzel was the first one up and did a hard workout and finished just as Madison went to start. They smiled as they passed but didn't say anything. The blonde told herself it was because he was so sweaty and she wanted to focus on her workout, having just done all her stretches.

Yasmeen slept little but well. She missed looking out of her window back home as soon as she woke up in her high-rise apartment. She did some light Pilates and then decided to think about what she was going to write on her blog when she was out. The Florida-born 29-year-old wondered what sponsors she could get on board and what products she could promote. And how best to do her interview once she had finished. In one large chunk with a feedback session afterwards, in themed bits or letting them ask questions and the best ones could be answered in advance? She started lining up the pros and cons of each.

Nate had been playing video games since he woke up, even forgetting about his cereal. Even before the Knicks, the 31-year-old loved playing as Mario, Sonic, Link or Ryu. His dream as a kid had been to be a video game player, creator, test gamer, voice character, whatever. He remembered how hard his parents had worked to be able to buy him a new game. When they died, he took out all the jokes that affectionately referenced them. He missed them. The Queens native wished he could hug Zeus. He wanted his brown and white pug to have a good time with his neighbour but not so good he would forget him.

Although they had started eating alone, either in the main room or in their room, the four had started taking meals together. When Nate had gone for his cereal, he was almost tempted to look for the others. But he knew everyone had their own routine at breakfast. While it was obvious that Yasmeen was losing out most from the lack of a fixed routine, Nate had struggled enough without sports. Taking out meat would make it even harder. The first thing he was going to do was order a Kung Pao chicken from the Chinese takeaway exactly 400 metres from his apartment.

After a power nap, Denzel awoke and decided to surprise everyone by making a meal for them all. The 37-year-old had checked with the others if his spaghetti recipe was good. Even retired, he still loved his carbs. Yasmeen had some specific requirements that needed ingredients to be sent for. They arrived in plenty of time, with a note from Selina as to why each brand for each ingredient was the best. That woman sure did love her detail, chuckled Denzel to himself as he started to cook.

Madison heard him cooking and decided to help. Denzel usually preferred being alone in the kitchen, but Madison was all right by him. He knew how loaded she was and figured she'd be super stuck up, but he'd been impressed by her. And the fact she was useful in the kitchen was always worth points.

For the most part, the talk was about how insane the process was and how they imagined their family would be watching it. Afterwards, Yasmeen went to her room to work on Spanish and continue her plans for after the process. Madison and Denzel decided to watch a film and after playfully fighting over what to watch, settled on *Ghost*.

It happened a couple of times that Denzel went to say something and then stopped and just smiled at her. Denzel thought Madison hadn't noticed, but she had. Surprised by how such a confident guy seemed quiet, the blonde 41-year-old spoke first. "You know, I gotta ask something." She looked him intently in the eyes.

Denzel looked away from the screen and back at her. "Sure."

"Did you finish the left-over cookies on the first night? I've been really curious who it was."

Denzel laughed. "That was not what I thought you were going to ask. But yeah, it was me."

Madison playfully threw a cushion at him.

"I thought there was more," reasoned the 37-year-old Denzel. "I know Nate eats a lot when he's writing so figured he'd have some more in his room. Besides, I made it up with that kick-ass lasagna I made tonight."

"What made you choose it?" she asked, intrigued.

"Well, I knew if it was spaghetti, Nate would get it all over his chin. You know I ain't wrong." They both laughed. "My man's alright, though. Fun guy."

"Being a stand-up is almost in Nate's blood. Would you ever go on stage? You're a confident guy," said Madison inquisitively.

"I could be confident. It doesn't mean I'd be good," laughed Denzel. "My parents wanted me to be an actor. That's why they called me Denzel. Brother really can act. Me, not so much. I never felt I belonged on stage."

"Did you ever seriously try it?" asked Madison softly.

"Once," he said after a long pause. "But it took me too damn long to remember the lines, and I didn't enjoy being on stage. I felt I was being watched, which I know sounds dumb, but I felt really awkward and uncomfortable. I didn't want to escape into a character. I just wanted to be me. The best version of me.

"On the field, it all just came so easy," he continued. "Well, not too easy at first. I had to work really hard on my physique and on my athletic skills. People forget that. My parents weren't thrilled, but they came along after they realised how serious I was about it. They both read up on coaching. Especially my mum." Denzel burst out laughing, a face full of proud joy as he tapped his chest. "The way she talked to my coaches. Always had my back."

"High school must have been a fun time for you," said Madison smiling. "Big jock on campus with that Hercules physique."

"Ah, I lived like a king," replied Denzel wistfully. "I kept pushing to see how much I could get away, and the teachers kept letting me. No matter what I did, they rarely said anything, and there was never any real punishment."

"Try being an heiress with New York's best lawyers on speed dial," chuckled Madison. "I was such a brat when I was younger. Ungrateful and unpleasant. Like I was the only one with problems."

Madison poured herself another glass, finishing the bottle. Denzel was still on his fifth can of beer.

"Something tells me you did ok at school with your looks," said Denzel flirtatiously.

At that moment was the pottery scene. Denzel went to grab the remote off of her, but she resisted. "Oh, come on, no way I'm watching this," Denzel said with a grin.

"I'll let you watch the original *Road House* later," reasoned Madison. "Patrick Swayze's in it, so totally fair!"

They both laughed and suddenly realised how close they were to each other. They stared into each other's eyes for a moment and moved in closer, their lips about to touch.

"I'm a genius," shouted Nate as he walked into the room, blissfully unaware of what he was interrupting. "Guess who just finished his latest comedy sketch? That's right, me!" He did a little twirl. "Hey, scootch over, this scene is hilarious," he said as he sat down between them and started mimicking the pottery using a glass of water.

"Hey, what's going on," called out Yasmeen as she entered. "You guys seem in a good mood. Wow, I've not seen *Ghost* in years."

And the truth was, it was as happy as they had been since they walked into that waiting room.

And then, the klaxon sounded.

Eden, such as it was, went back to hell. The four scattered as they went to sort their things out. They knew the drill well enough by now. Anything on their bed would come with them, anything not on or by the bed would be left and then destroyed. Denzel had made Nate's bed (or "lazy ass slob" as he often called him) so it didn't take long for their stuff to be ready. Having already mediated and practiced Pilates earlier, Yasmeen spent time looking at her drawings, before leaving a large note on her bed saying, "This show is dumb".

And then before long, they were stood in line. Nate was still grinning, but the others were in stony silence. Yasmeen took the hand of Madison; Madison took the hand of Denzel and Denzel hesitated and then reluctantly grabbed Nate's hand before thinking better of it and letting it go.

And the four walked into the studio, the lights as dazzling and the noise as startling as ever. And Buck on stage, bouncing off the energy of the crowd, just as he loved it.

"Welcome back, you wonderful people," he said with the boundless energy of someone in kindergarten. "I know we've kept you waiting a little longer this time. "I know, we're sneaky like that. But you don't become rebels by following the rules. And we're definitely rule-breakers. What other gameshow is doing what we're doing with our level of preparation and intrigue?"

There was a silence, which was then filled by Buck's infectious laugh. "Well, don't worry, I missed you all, too. I know you've been desperate to see who's next. Let's go and meet the four again."

Buck was a manic ball of energy as he went down the steps and in front of the four. "Hey, Nate the Great, as you've been called by your fans. Or the Nateteniers. Their word, not mine. Your new fan club has been loving your jokes since you've been here. I have a question for you. Are you still chill?"

Nate smiled and grabbed the microphone off of Buck, pointing to his shirt that had a picture of a polar bear with a beer. "You know me, I'm the Big Chill. Nothing fazes me. I'll be fine.

Buck grinned. "Well, if you're the Big Chill, I guess that makes me the Big Buck. I can live with that! What about you, Denzel? How are you finding things?"

"I'm focused. I spent years training for big moments, so I'm good," replied Denzel. And he was confident. The experts who had been analysing in forensic detail the body language of each contestant could see just how disciplined he was.

"Madison, Madison, Madison, those cookies you baked sure looked delicious," said Buck. "I could practically reach out and touch them. Or was that just me?" The crowd roared in agreement. "But we do have to ask, were they better than your own family's? In fact, we've got the two together and you can do a blindfolded test."

There was a slight look of panic and seeing her expression, Denzel went to say something but, that's when Buck started laughing. "I'm kidding, but wow, the look on your face!" And he was still laughing, in that snazzy orange suit, when he moved on to Yasmeen.

"You know, Yasmeen, you're the most mysterious of all the contestants. You're edgy and rebellious and yet you also have moments of calm and ya know, serenity. Which is the real you?

"They're both me."

"And have you enjoyed your time on the show so far?

"Not really. Kinda sucks."

"Well, people, the punk princess thinks it sucks," said Buck with a sigh. "I gotta say, I'm loving it. And I definitely know you guys out there are loving it, too. There's been a 12% increase in voting since last time." He pointed to the predictions table. "That definitely does not suck."

Madison was far out in front with 34.2%, Nate was second with 25.2%, Denzel third with 23.5% and Yasmeen fourth with 17.1%.

Suddenly the voting stopped, and the names and colours were chosen.

Denzel Harker: Red 1
Yasmeen Kahley: White 4

Nate Reeder: Yellow 5
Madison Larouch: Green 6

As always, the lights in the studio changed and the music started.

"That's my cue, boys," exclaimed Buck with great relish. "It's showtime." And with that, he started to spin. "Spin to win, spin to lose, who gets what, the board will choose," and the board kept whirling round. Madison found herself feeling dizzy and, desperate to avoid looking at the board or the crowd, looked to the others. Nate was clapping along, Denzel looked like he was waiting for the game whistle to start, and Yasmeen looked as though she was somewhere else altogether.

Their thought processes were broken up by the screaming voice of Buck. "It's slowing down, it's slowing down!" And the answer was only moments away.

"It's Denzel!" shouted Buck as the wheel stopped. The bright lights were on the 37-year-old to capture every aspect of his reaction. The former athlete breathed in heavily several times, but his posture remained straight, and there was stoic determination. Nate and Yasmeen's expressions barely changed, but Madison looked like she was fighting back tears.

"Well, Denzel, it's bad news for you. The party's over, big man! You need to head to that exit. No return ticket! Anything you want to say to everyone here in the studio and watching back home all over the world?"

"I can do this! I will do this! And go, Giants!" he said with quiet determination. And he looked at Madison with a sad smile, who looked back at him for a split second before she had to turn away. At that moment, they looked to the screen, where it was playing Denzel's interview made before it all started.

"Hi, I'm Denzel "Maverick" Harker. I'm 37, born and bred in my hometown of Philly and I used to be a tight end for the New York Giants. And yes, with them I won the Super Bowl. That moment will always be with me!" He kissed his ring and pointed it out to the camera in a big show of energy.

"Y'all know I'm from Philadelphia, and if you told me that a kid who grew up in Hunting Park, whose old man died from a stroke when I was 10, would grow up to be one of the most famous athletes in America, I sure as hell wouldn't have believed you. My career ended sooner than I'd have liked, but I ain't complaining. It was a good career, and I know my old man would have been proud of me for my life on the field."

Madison was smiling. There really was so much that she didn't know about him. Nate was watching with bemused interest, with Yasmeen was also paying attention, though pretending she wasn't.

The confident tone of Denzel changed as he started the next part of the interview. "I know I ain't the smartest. I've made mistakes. I know I've hurt people. People I cared about. After I retired early because of my injury, I was not a good person. I behaved badly. I was not a good role model for my kids Caleb, Aniyah and Ayden. I let my family down, I let my former teammates down, I let God down. I'm ashamed of that drunk driving charge. I paid for the kid's treatment, but the fact he can't walk properly now is something I will feel for the rest of my life. I know there were women. I lied to them, told them all they wanted to hear."

There was a long pause, and he looked away from the camera. "The sex tape stuff. I ain't proud. I was in a bad place. The girl did say it was alright to film her on the night, even though she said different after. I shouldn't have sent it on to friends though, and I get why she was so upset after. I never meant for it to go to so many people. And I want it clear, I never wanted to make money off her or blackmail her. It was just an empty threat. Just a lot went wrong, and I'm sorry. I want y'all to see the real me. I want to make my kids proud of me again."

Madison was stony-faced as she slowly looked away from the screen and into the eyes of Denzel. Though he was far from her usual type, there had been something magnetic about the muscular former American football player. With his flair for cooking, his ambition to go against his parents' wishes and his positive energy and confident outlook, she thought there was more to him and had sensed a spark. But she was done with him. Both Nate and Yasmeen noticed the look.

Denzel's shoulders slumped further as he was led away. Having been one of the most popular contestants, it was clear that not everyone in the studio was aware of how bad his mistakes had been. But spelt out in the cold light of day, there was no hiding from it. And his night was only going to get worse.

Like with the previous two, he soon found himself in a car with guards blocking any hint of an exit. As chiselled and toned as Denzel was, it was clear he would not win in a battle with the security team. Perhaps if he hadn't seen the way Madison's face had dropped when watching the video, he might have had the energy to try. Not so long ago, he was about to kiss a gorgeous, smart, rich woman who seemed to see the best in him. He hadn't even cared she was loaded. Damn that short-ass nerd and his lousy timing. Now, the 6 foot 4 Philadelphian felt he could barely lift his own shoulders.

He hadn't even begun to think about the challenge. Unlike Jed, he hadn't deliberately hidden his phobia, but he didn't still like talking about it with people. Being in a locker room with a bunch of alpha males the less they knew about your weaknesses the better. Ah, he still missed the game so much.

He was so in his own world that he didn't hear a mobile ring or it being answered. Suddenly one of the security guards handed him a phone with a voice he knew all too well.

"Good evening, Denzel," welcomed the cold voice of Selina. "Your time in the house is up, and your challenge will await you soon."

Denzel said nothing, just looked into the windows he was unable to see out of as they were tinted, just like with the two previous contestants. Seeing there would be no response, Selina continued. "You will arrive at the chosen location in about 10 minutes. There, you will sleep, and then you will take the final step of this process before you can leave."

Seeing as Denzel didn't say anything, she hung up. She wasn't sure if he had really heard her, but she wouldn't waste any time thinking about it. She had plenty to be getting on with, including a big interview with a major radio station.

Without a watch, Denzel had no idea if it was ten minutes or ten hours. He was torn between wanting to get the challenge over right away and having time to recover his game face. The former tight-end was trying to be positive, even if it wasn't coming naturally. He saw the look Madison had given him. It was the same look his coach had given him when Denzel had fumbled the ball just before the endzone, costing them a shot at the playoffs. A mixture of disappointment, disgust and fury.

It took him a while to sleep in his new surroundings, a small room with little in the way of decoration. Denzel was used to the best of hotels in his time as a professional athlete. Here was a reminder of life before all that. Bad art, noisy air vents and a small bed that barely covered his feet.

Denzel was a natural sleeper, something that always came in handy on game nights. Now though, lots of thoughts were running through his head. It had been nice being around people who didn't really know about his background. About his screwups. They just saw him as 'Maverick', who kept in shape, cooked kick-ass food and was fun to be around. Not as the guy who had made bad choices over a couple of years and gone to therapy far later than he should have done. After a while, he began to feel light-headed and soon fell asleep.

He awoke by hitting his head, having felt some weird movement around him. Denzel had always been a jump out of bed, draw the curtains and burst into song kind of guy, but this time something had stopped him. As he opened his eyes properly, if a little groggily, he realised how much trouble he was in. It was dark and cramped. He had no space to move his arms, legs or anything. To his horror, Denzel realised he was in a coffin.

"Arghhhhhhhhhhhhhhhhhhhhhhhhhhhhhhhhhhhhhhhhhhhhhhhhhhhhhhh hh! Get me out of this! This isn't funny. I can't do this. Please don't make me do this. I can't! I really can't."

He banged so heavily and screamed so loud he would have woken anyone who wasn't already dead. At least, if the unseen microphones in his coffin hadn't already been set to a lower volume. Concerned about his screaming being unpopular with viewers, Selina had calculated the level it would shock the audience without going to a level where people would complain.

She had also anticipated things by adding a note about the likelihood of cursing. Which was just as well, as the swearing didn't stop until his knuckles started to bleed and his words became garbled. Going the extra mile, she'd make sure no matter what noise he made, Denzel would always be able to hear anything going on from outside his coffin. And for those who wanted to see his agony visually, the cameras had been fitted in, both in colour and black and white. Not to mention the running commentary of celebrity doctor, Denis Kavolkan, who had been invited back after the unexpected success of his first two outings.

And he was perfectly capturing Denzel's terror, with insights referencing different quotes and theories of Freud, Jung and Pavlov, among more modern names. As before, the other commentary available was jokey and asking all kinds of themed random questions. Everything from which would be the most inconvenient snack to eat in a coffin to which celebrity would cope best and people's favourite vampire.

Denzel couldn't stand up; he couldn't move around. One of his first thoughts had been to try and topple over the coffin, but he was wedged in and could barely move. It was dark and quiet, and he was alone. He didn't care what the other two challenges had been. There was no way the previous two could be worse than being in the dark and unable to swing his wrists. Denzel Harker may not have been dead, but he was praying for it. Hell couldn't be any worse than this.

Suddenly, there were sounds. He could hear it. By the timing of the footprints, it seemed that two different people had entered the room.

"You know, he was one hell of an NFL player," said a gruff voice full of nostalgic passion. "I know you're not into sports, but that kid was something special before all the injuries. I remember that Super Bowl final from 2012. He was unplayable that night. Pure carnage."

Thinking he was saved, Denzel had been banging and shouting again at the top of his lungs. And yet they couldn't hear him. How could they not hear him? He was screaming loud enough to wake the dead. Why were they acting like he was the one dead? Surely, his being in the box was the challenge. He was petrified of enclosed spaces.

"Yeah, the guy was in shape," said a youthful voice. "Totally ripped."

"I never even knew he had any heart troubles," said the older voice in a more solemn tone. "Just dying in his sleep like that. Thought that stuff was pretty rare."

As the two continued talking, Denzel zoned out. Dying in his sleep? That was for old people. Sick people. People with no passion or energy. He had been fine when he'd gone to sleep that night. There was no history of heart trouble in the family. Well, only his grandfather, but that's because he stuffed himself every night and smoked and drank himself to an early grave.

So many questions were floating round his head manically. How could his heart have stopped beating? He would have remembered dying. How could he have come back to life? Why couldn't they hear him? Perhaps most important of all was one that kept swirling around in his head. How long could he survive? Without water, air. How long could he stay sane?

Denzel realised he should start paying attention to what they were saying.

"Just as well," said the older voice. "The way you dropped that coffin when you were moving it earlier. Like King Kong with a bar of soap."

"Nah, I'm more like Thor baby. You should see the size of my hammer."

"Honestly, Marlon. Show some respect for the dead."

Denzel gulped before banging even harder. The same voice continued unaffected. "Don't forget, a mourner wants to stop by. I know the family agreed on a closed casket, but I've promised her I'd open it so she could say goodbye properly. She missed the funeral earlier. Didn't leave a name or say how she knew him."

"How much did she give you?"

"I didn't charge her! Honestly, Marlon, you're in the wrong industry."

As Marlon began to talk about how attractive Denzel's ex-girlfriends were, how it would feel to win a Super Bowl, and how he could get his physique if he didn't like doughnuts, Denzel just wanted him to shut up. Just how long would he have to wait? If he could stay sane, he would be saved. He just had to hold on.

And yet they couldn't hear him. After he stopped banging, he paid more attention to the conversation. The younger guy was still talking. "Come on, dude had no personality. Just money and a six-pack. I'm going to join a gym after I leave tonight."

"You think you could get in better shape than a former NFL Super Bowl winner?" was the incredulous reply.

"Well, I'm breathing, ain't I? So, I'm already doing better than him!" was the waspish response. What made it even funnier to viewers was that the young man was already muscular. Rather than the lazy, slobbish couch potato Denzel was imagining, Marlon (Troy in regular life) was a serious athlete who had recently finished fifth in his last Iron Man competition. Marlon wasn't related to Gerald (or Colin), his slightly older co-star. In fact, the two had never worked together. But they had clicked in auditions and were vibing well on live TV.

"Besides, I don't reckon it was the faulty heart that killed him," continued Marlon. "It was the idea of facing those spiders. At least he died before he had to do the challenge. And they said he was dumb." Marlon laughed as he drank a Coke.

"Don't be too hard on him," countered Gerald. "He's not the only guy who hates spiders. They give me the creeps. I wonder what the challenge actually was. They've not said anything."

This deliberately misleading information answered something that had been buzzing inside Denzel's head. If this wasn't the challenge, then what was it? Hearing the talk of spiders answered it once and for all. He'd once mentioned in an interview a teammate had once left a tarantula in his locker and he'd had to get his own back.

"Life is weird," he found himself shouting with all manner of curse words. "Because they thought I was afraid of something I was going to do some messed up challenge I wasn't actually afraid of. But because I'm now dead, or not quite dead, I gotta do an even worse one!" Life sucked big time. In life, in death, and in this messed-up bit in the middle.

"I could have faked it," he said to himself out loud. "I mean, I don't like spiders. Which freak would? But it would have been better than this."

Denzel was still struggling to come to terms with that and everything else. It was like he was a ghost. Not ghosting like the countless times he had failed to respond to women after sleeping with them, but what ghosting should really mean. Powerless to be seen or heard when life was happening all around you.

"Well, it was a good send-off," said Gerald with a reflective sigh. As Denzel would never see him, the audition had focused less on his appearance and more on his voice. It was a real break for the 55-year-old Gerald, who was 6 foot five, thin, pale and much to his disappointment, never a consideration for leading man status. But he did have a good voice and had had a solid career doing voiceovers and being understudies. He was going to enjoy his moment in the sun and see where it took him. "It was a lovely service, really. I don't know why that lady had to make those comments, though. Interrupting the priest too. It was rather unnecessary."

"She was right, though," added Marlon. "And it wasn't like anyone disagreed. I always found him to be fake. And a bit of a jackass."

Considering he was supposed to be dead; it was all rather disrespectful.

Denzel was trying to work out who this woman was and what she had said. Of course, there had been no service, no woman and no controversy. Watching Denzel going through his life to try and figure out who the woman could be was later voted one of the highlights of the evening.

Second only to Denzel realising he didn't have his Super Bowl ring. That offensive talk had made him come back to something that always earned him respect. And as he reached out to hold it, it was gone. Denzel had felt fear and he had felt confusion, now it was just rage.

"No one disrespects me like that! No one! I earned that ring with blood, sweat and tears. I gave everything I had, and they remove it like it was trash!"

His rant was interrupted by Marlon. "You know, I think this Super Bowl ring is gonna give me magical powers." He held it in his hand. "Precious, my precious," he said in a Gollum impersonation from *Lord of The Rings*.

"Marlon," replied Gerald exasperated. "Can't you at least wait until you've finished eating? You've got ketchup all over it. And I think that's mustard too. At least use a napkin."

"Gerald, Gerald, I'm a smart guy remember… Where's the mayo? Oh, there it is. Yeah, this baby is so gonna get me laid. I'm going to do some travelling around South America. I'm gonna get more action than a piñata at a siesta."

"That's a fiesta, genius. Siesta is the one where you nap."

"Nah, I'll leave the napping to Denzel."

Viewers could see the rage in Denzel's face. If the coffin hadn't been reinforced with extra wood, he might well have bashed through it and then sent Marlon across the room with a punch. That rage was glorious, and even comical, as he couldn't even extend his arms properly. One cartoonist later drew him as a five-year-old full of rage being held off while Marlon was still eating a sandwich (with a dirty Super Bowl ring for added effect).

But it was all part of the process. And now it was time to ramp it up.

"Clean yourself up, we're going to cremate him soon," said Gerald, and Denzel instantly changed from screaming from rage to fear. A cremation meant being burned alive. Unless someone could hear him, he was going to be burned to a crisp. It was starting to sink in.

"I'm getting my playlist ready," said Marlon enthusiastically. "We've got half an hour until the cremation service starts. Plenty of time for my funky playlist. Let me see. 'Disco Inferno' by The Trammps, then onto 'Fire' by Kasabian, 'I'm on Fire' by Bruce Springsteen, 'Light My Fire' by the Doors, 'Eternal Flame' by The Bangles, then 'Ring of Fire' by Johnny Cash and finishing with 'The Heat is On' by Glen Frey."

Selina hadn't managed to get the music labels on board immediately, but then she was a convincing person. And with so many famous songs about heat, she had plenty of leverage. As she predicted, all of the songs later sailed up the chart.

None of which was helping Denzel. He had been desperate for death earlier. But not like this. What a rotten way to die. He'd long stopped banging. It was clear they couldn't hear him and were never going to. But at least he had hope. That mourner was going to come along, and they'd promised to open the casket.

"So, who's this person arriving later?" asked Marlon. "Anyone hot? Grieving women are always easier. And black lace is sexy."

"Calm it," said Gerald, sounding unimpressed but unsurprised. "She mentioned that she was a personal trainer but couldn't get out of her session as she had an important client. Said she would be running a little late as her client arrived late due to the roads being dug up."

Denzel found himself talking out loud again. "That's it. It's not fair. I don't deserve this rotten luck. Where's my good luck? Roadworks! I can't catch a break. I don't deserve this. I never killed anyone. Never hit someone who didn't deserve it. I worked hard and gave everything on the field. Everything. I bought my momma a new house when I could afford it. I never hazed any of the new players. I was helpful to those getting injured. I never disrespected the jersey, even when I played for rival teams after the injuries started."

He went quiet again as he tried not to cry.

"She messaged to say her class is over and she's heading over. Sounds a local," said Gerald.

"Just give me five minutes' notice before she arrives so I can put on a smarter shirt," said Marlon.

"You'll need more than five minutes for that," said Gerald with a chuckle. "She's sent a photo, so I'll recognise her. You'll definitely like her. If I were younger, I'd have nudged you out of the way and distracted you with different condiments."

"Nothing wrong with having a healthy appetite," said the unabashed Marlon. "Besides, we'll all be in a shoebox one day."

"True," said Gerald with a profound air. "It makes you think. I mean, here was a big-time celebrity who won the biggest prize in his sport early on in his career. And yet, apart from his mother and his sister, the words were all rather underwhelming. None of his teammates had much anything too memorable to say about him, even in the press. Just that he was a good player when fit and an ok guy to have in the locker room. Makes you think, doesn't it?"

"Yeah, he'll be forgotten soon enough," replied his younger colleague. "Some lump will kick the ball further than him, and he'll be yesterday's news."

Hearing this, Denzel went very quiet. He'd always thought his teammates would speak well of him. He'd always pretended to like them. When Shawn Jackson had that serious injury, Denzel really did act concerned. When players were dropped, Denzel pretended to care about the ones in his position as much as the other parts of the team. When he retired, he made sure to speak well of them all in public. That should have been enough for some really nice words. What more did they want?

It took him a few minutes to regain his composure. So much so that he missed Gerald's explanation of what a tight end does, as well as a basic explanation of how American Football works. Instead, the conversation returned to more poignant topics.

"Come on, he'll leave more of a legacy than a big bank account and nice suits?" pleaded Gerald. "Surely?"

"Oh yeah, the suits," reasoned Marlon in a calculated voice. "I reckon I can nab some later on. Not like his family will be checking his wardrobe too much."

Gerald and Marlon were then given strict instructions not to say anything that might influence what Denzel would say next. There was a gap of several minutes while Denzel thought long and hard. For the first time in his life, Denzel was looking at his life in third person. Without distractions and without anyone to influence his thoughts.

"You know me, God, I ain't all bad," said Denzel out loud after a long period of reflection. "I never killed anyone. And that thing with the boy was an accident. I would never have had those drinks if I thought there would be any pedestrians about. I mean, it was after midnight."

There was a pause, as though Denzel had said everything to say on that topic and was now moving on to a new paragraph.

"I guess I could have treated women better. I mean, they did throw themselves at me, but yeah, I could have called them back when I told them I was going to. Once I had the kids, I did cut back. It's important to set a good example. I'd have been a better dad. The fun but protective kind. I'd have planned all these amazing birthday parties, not just made sure I got them a good present when their mother reminded me. I'd have done so much for them.

"And I'd tell them to avoid what I did wrong. That video stuff was bad. One day they're gonna read about it. Thing was, I didn't even mean to send the video to the guys. Then, I didn't wanna admit it, and I just couldn't back down. I ain't a bad guy. I'm good. Just stupid sometimes. I'm sorry, I'm sorry."

And then he began to cry. The loud, wailing kind he'd never done before. "I hope you're proud of me, Dad. I did good, too. Don't forget the good things I did. I missed you so much when you passed." And Denzel realised he couldn't stop crying.

Waiting a few minutes to be sure Denzel had finished talking, the music stopped, and Marlon's voice called out. "You know, this almost burns as high as 1500 degrees. I don't even like taking something out of the oven when it's 150!"

"Wait a second," said Gerald. "It's the neighbour."

Denzel was going to be rescued. Some hot stranger was going to come in and save him. He didn't care who she was. Or what she looked like. He was just so grateful. He was in hell, but he had found the exit door just in time. His efforts to stay sane had all been worth it. He readied himself for the moment of salvation.

"That's odd," said Gerald in a surprised tone. As instructed by Selina, he waited a long time for dramatic effect. The cameras fully captured Denzel's joy turning to confusion and then the slight hints of worry.

"Sometime today would be nice," responded Marlon in a tone dripping with sarcasm.

"I'll read it out." Gerald changed to a more formal voice. "Thank you for agreeing to meet me so I could say my final farewell to Denzel. I didn't know him well but wanted that closure. He was so handsome, so charming. I had such fun with him. We were both married, so we knew it wouldn't last, but we had a great time. Waiting in the car park, it hit me that I should not see him. I need to respect his family's wishes for privacy. If Denzel had ever wanted more, he would have told me. I need to respect him and his family and get closure through this message."

"What a waste, though," exclaimed the younger man. "I bet she had a banging body. Read that part again about..."

"She's deleted it," responded Gerald. "As soon as she saw I'd read it. Probably realised she shouldn't be that honest with people she'd never met. Ah well, once he's incinerated, we can all move on."

That was the final straw for Denzel. He began screaming louder than he thought possible, until suddenly he went quiet. That's when Serena said something into the earphones of Marlon and Gerald, who immediately pulled Denzel out. Rather than the rage or relief they had been expecting, they struggled to get him out of the box. Not because he was exhausted but because he was catatonic.

It was going to be a long road back for Denzel, if at all.

Intermission

Things were quiet at the house. Madison had immediately gone to the room and closed the door. Rightly assuming she'd want to be alone, Yasmeen and Nate had stayed out of her way. Nate was playing video games in the main lounge while Yasmeen was reading in the guys' room. With Denzel's things being removed, the room felt eerily empty, even if Nate had continued his messy tradition by throwing his clothes on the floor when changing and leaving empty food packets around.

Madison was struggling with a whole array of emotions. In the few hours since coming back, she had seemed to go through at least half a dozen. Anger for how he treated that woman and quite clearly others like her. Embarrassment for almost falling for his charms. Relief that she hadn't. Guilt that she had got lucky. Confusion as to why she had fallen for him in the first place. And frustration that she was back to square one on the dating board. She lay on her bed and put on a playlist without really listening to it.

While this was going on, Selina was in a studio, waiting for her interview. She didn't like the idea of being the centre of attention, but she did like success and was determined to spark a new batch of column inches and online debate. The Harvard maths graduate had run all the numbers and analysed all the data. She was keen to avoid TV or anything visual but an radios and podcasts were fine. She felt more in control, less on show. It was her voice that viewers liked most, anyhow. A few promotional photos would be needed, and that was okay. Being a district swimming champion, she was used to being photographed. What she didn't want was people analysing her body language. It was vital she still had control.

She'd painstakingly researched all the most popular shows that struck that balance of street cred and journalistic integrity and narrowed it down to three. *Mickey and the Brain*, an irreverent take on current events, hosted by a wacky carpenter and his inquisitive and cerebral Princeton graduate best friend. *Rock Around the Clock*, where you chose your five favourite albums to take on a desert island, but really it was just an excuse to talk about your latest promotional activity. And *Incision*, a podcast by a highly perceptive dentist-turned-journalist who mixed hard-hitting questions with wince-inducing puns.

Incision it was.

And so she sat patiently in the lounge of the small but comfortable studio, waiting for the interview to start. She'd listened to his first five shows, as well as his last twelve, so knew his style well. It wasn't about catching you off guard or getting you angry. It really was just about asking the right questions and letting the interviewee speak. The style of two contrary guests desperate to speak over each other was effective but wasn't hers. She had to be in control, even when she wasn't supposed to be. Thanks to Eric's marketing guru of a husband, she didn't have to worry about promoting anything herself. Malcolm had been so innovative in his use of social media since she arranged the interview, she was considering hiring him. Amongst cute photos of him and Eric together, there was excellent analysis of failed marketing campaigns, detailed insight into important hirings and firings within major brands and humorous but perceptive takes on rapid changes taking place within consumer behaviour.

"Hi, Selina, nice to meet you" said the warm, comforting voice of Eric Cho. Selina looked up to see the smiling face of Cho, who brushed his dark hair aside and fiddled with his glasses in a slightly shy manner before offering his hand for a handshake.

"Thank you, Mr Cho," responded Selina.

"Eric is fine," chuckled the amiable host as he looked at his Rolex and gestured for her to sit opposite him. As he prepared his notes, a young assistant handed her a glass of water and checked the seat was the right height and the microphone was in the perfect position.

Eric breathed out while waiting for the countdown.

"Hello and welcome to another edition of *Incision*, the programme where we drill down a guest to find out all the behind-the-scenes information. I've been rooting around in my gameshow notes and brushing up on the social media feedback, so I've warned our next guest to brace herself for some sharp questions. Okay, okay no more of my dentist puns, let me introduce her."

Selina hadn't laughed at any of his jokes, but that wasn't uncommon from any of his guests.

"I'm here with Selina Stevenson, the youngest-ever head in the history of the IPPR TV network when she was appointed seven years ago. Indeed, Stevenson is the youngest ever female on a nationwide TV network and only the second youngest overall. In her time, the network once regarded as "a waste of space" and "king of the losers" by her predecessor, is currently third in the latest rankings, and who would bet against her working her magic still further to get the top? 'I set ambitious targets,' Stevenson once said. 'That's what life is all about. Aiming high and doing everything possible to achieve it.'"

Selina smiled modestly, as she remembered the interview.

"Stevenson's sharp industry insight and ruthless removal of underperforming but much-loved shows have seen her dubbed TV's "Golden Girl" and "The Queen of Mean," continued Cho, fully concentrated on reading his notes perfectly. "The Connecticut-born executive with a 4.0 average and Harvard degree in mathematics has never been shy of making a tough decision, nor of its fallout. Something that has stood her in good stead as IPPR's latest show *Wheel of Phobia* has not been off the front pages and social media since its introduction a week ago.

"For those precious few people who have been living under a rock, *Wheel of Phobia* has six former celebrities, or should we say disgraced celebrities, competing for $7.2 million. The twist, one of several twists really, is that in each episode a contestant gets knocked out if their name is randomly chosen by the wheel, before then facing their greatest phobia in a challenge specifically designed to take them to their limit. Despite, or because of the huge controversy, the show has been a ratings success, breaking viewing records and dominating the news. Tell me Selina, why do you think in a world where sport and scripted drama tend to get the highest ratings, a gameshow has been such a hit?"

"There are many reasons as to why the show has connected so many people," replied Selina with composed assurance. "The main one is that we don't insult the audience. All six of the celebrities have a profound phobia. It isn't some mild unpleasantness for them. When that wheel is spinning, however, they may be acting on the inside, each of the six is genuinely terrified. We ramp up the excitement, the drama, the anticipation. Other shows use a wheel to win money, we use it to take the contestants to their mental and emotional limits."

"There is still a big cash prize at stake."

"Yes, and the $7.2 million is far bigger than any other cash prize around. If you added all the other prizes from other conventional gameshows together, that still wouldn't even make a dent in ours. And unlike other traditional TV shows where the money is a possibility, ours is a certainty. One of those six will definitely be walking out with the cash prize. And they won't even have had to answer a trivia question or undertake a challenge. There's nothing else in TV like it. And don't forget it's live, so no edits. Viewers can see everything that happens as it happens."

"So why do you think the six took part?" ventured Eric. "How much of it is the money? I mean, Madison's family is the 21st richest family in the country. "

"I really think the money is only a small part," said Selina. "Each will have their own motives, but I think they want to be loved again. And respected. To be relevant again. And we are giving them that chance. What stands out in their interviews is that they have had chances. This isn't their second or third or even fourth chance. This is their last salvation. The public had given up on them. And once that happens, it's almost impossible to get back. That's really why they've signed up for the show."

"How hard was it to convince them to sign up?"

"Well, we had a lot of leverage. They may be less-than-popular celebrities now, but these aren't stars who lost their lustre because of a few lousy albums or poor film choices. They didn't fall out of the public eye because they focused on family life or needed some time to cope away from the spotlight. They made big mistakes that the public has found hard to forgive. But the six love all the perks that come with being famous, and they're desperate to get it back. And I think we have to be fair and say, these are resilient people. It takes a lot to take the shots they have taken and still put yourself out there. After what all of them have gone through, it would have been easy for them to settle for an easy life. Sure, they've made a lot of mistakes, but to willingly sign up and put yourself in a situation where you're most vulnerable, I respect them, and I think the audience does too."

"They may have signed up willingly, but that hasn't stopped some serious allegations they are being exploited," probed Eric. "You'll be aware of the huge backlash the show has faced since its launch. To quote the Santa Fame charity, who dedicate themselves to former celebrities who have addiction and financial battles, you 'milk the contestants until they moo with pain.'"

"If they're going to paraphrase Dorothy Parker's famous quote, it's only fair to quote her."

"Be that as it may, what is your response to such a serious allegation?" continued Eric in a firmer tone. "The columnist Malcolm Glinder said. 'You dangle them by their tails like rats in a maze before setting the cats on them.' Glenda Johnson at rival network TPAT called the show 'dangerous, shameful and sick'. Those are some strong words."

"They are, but that doesn't mean they are the correct words," said Selina passionately. "I resent the rats analogy. The accommodation is clean and tidy, they have regular meals with all diets and allergies considered. There are all kinds of entertainment devices tailor-made for them."

"I do believe he meant more about the voyeuristic element rather than the more practical living arrangements," clarified Eric in a neutral tone.

"I understand, but when language is that loaded, it's important for me to clarify every possible interpretation. As for what you called voyeuristic, that's what TV is all about, especially when it comes to celebrities. We're fascinated by them. That's why so many magazines and websites give them so much coverage. What we're offering is the chance to see these people up close and personal. Unfiltered, uncensored and previously unimaginable. Sure, a lot of the debate is about the challenges, but viewing figures have been high throughout all the days. According to our feedback, people love watching celebrities interact with each other, as well as getting an idea of how they spend their time, including each person's specific creative processes or how they relax. These aren't random contestants who we'll forget about in a week's time."

"Do you ever feel sorry for the contestants?" queried Eric, shifting tone slightly. "Laronda Johnson, a former co-star of Linda Mayes, has said she wasn't able to enjoy it as she felt it was 'cruel and unkind punishment'. That's interesting as Johnson and Mayes fell out during the making of *Lost Sweethearts* and there's clearly no love between them as Johnson has pointed out in numerous interviews since *Wheel of Phobia* started. Don't you find that telling?"

"I find it telling that Johnson's last four films have made a huge loss, and my industry connections have told me she's just been removed from two separate projects," said Selina in a cutting tone, undercut with a sharp smile. "She might want to focus more on her career than mine. I'd also add that Johnson's comments about Linda over the years would very much qualify as cruel and unkind."

"Are you referring to the 'inbred Tennessee airhead' comment?"

"Yes, and the spineless carrot," added the TV executive.

"Johnson did apologise for those," noted Eric, immediately.

"Yes, eventually."

"Those were deeply unpleasant insults. But what would you say to those who feel that terrifying someone so much that their face goes white and they lose the power to speak is too far?"

"Terror isn't always bad," argued Selina. "Rollercoasters, haunted houses, scary movies. People are okay with being afraid."

"Not all people."

"Yes, not all people," remarked Selina as she sat further up in her chair in readiness to clarify her point. "Not all people like TV. Not all people are interested in celebrities. So, the 'not all people' thing isn't the issue for me. Why does everyone have to agree on everything? The best forms of creativity create a big reaction in its audience. I believe the biggest enemy of creativity is indifference. Some people will think we go too far, others won't think we go far enough. I believe in what we're doing, as do most viewers, so I can live with complaints from a small minority."

"Feedback saying you're not going far enough?" responded Eric, the surprise in his voice obvious. "I'm finding that hard to believe."

"For sure. Human beings aren't one entity. Each person has their own beliefs and way of thinking. The bigger the audience, the bigger the feedback, and it's important we try to consider everyone. My point is, we are more interested in the ones who turn up to the party ready to have a good time, rather than those who do nothing but complain and try to ruin the vibe for everyone else."

"So how do you know what is too far?" pondered Eric.

"We know."

"That's not really an answer."

"Well, it's not just me who decides," said Selina. "A lot of thought goes into each challenge. We also have psychologists on set. The actors have gestures they can use if they think it's gone too far."

"We'll get to the individual challenges in a moment. But first, I want to find out more about how this show got made. How did the initial idea come about? How involved were you with the original concept? I mean, there's a lot of people shocked this even got past its first meeting."

"An outline was proposed to me," answered Selina with a smile. "One of the things I insisted on when joining was more encouragement for new ideas. I hire more staff than anyone else to go through scripts. There's a quote by Murakami from *Norwegian Wood*. 'If you only read the same books that everyone else is reading, you can only think what everyone else is thinking.' I know you can read the same book to someone else and have a completely different take on it, but I get the overall point. You have to look in different places to offer something different. Every idea that gets sent to us, including those without an agent, gets read by at least two different people. The idea was sent to us by a previous unknown who knew it wouldn't get looked at by any of our competitors. That's why we were able to make it."

"Has the show's success surprised you?"

"A little," reflected Selina, after a moment's pause. "It's been higher than the projected numbers for sure. But we have some extremely talented people both behind the cameras and in front of them."

"The list of credits in each challenge only features the characters' names. It's very secretive. So, if I asked you for some of the names of those involved in the making of the show…"

"You wouldn't get very far," said a stony-faced Selina.

"I'll move on," remarked Etic with a rueful grin. "Devising a show where you specifically design a scenario where contestants have to face their greatest fear is certainly a controversial idea. There must have been some opposition behind the scenes."

"Of course. But whenever someone tries to do something different, push the boundary, go wildly where no one has gone before, there's pushback. People didn't want the Eiffel Tower built. Bohemian Rhapsody was deemed too long for radio stations. TV was a fad that would last six months tops. And it's important to not be one of those scared and ignorant people. There are no hapless passengers in IPPR, just pioneers. It's not about 'Can we do this?' it's about 'Let's Do This!'"

"Just to confirm," emphasised the interviewer. "You're saying there was no opposition within the company? Everyone was on board from the start?"

"Pretty much," grinned Selina. "Our legal team took a bit of persuading, as you can imagine. But nowhere near as much as you might think. The real opposition was from outside."

"Sponsors?"

"Yes," answered Selina, with purpose. "I get it. We are dealing with big brands, and they need to be cautious. We knew not all of them would be on board right away. But of the ones who initially said no, more than half have since signed up. As mentioned before, the numbers in everything have been high."

"You weren't worried about other external factors? Charities? Government? Religious groups? A social media backlash? The law?"

"That's not how we do things here," beamed Selina with pride. "If we believe the idea is strong enough, we go for it. We're adults. We knew we could handle it."

"Let's get on the individual challenges now," said Eric. "First off was Linda Mayes. Perhaps it was fitting that she went out first as she was the one who seemed to fall hardest before the show even started. From gap-toothed teenage starlet to credible artist, starring in Hollywood and singing for the president, to lurid tabloid details about how she cheated on her cancer-stricken husband, the so-called 'Mr Nicest Ever Guy', and proof that her charity was stealing money that was donated for terminally ill patients. Quite the fall from grace."

"She was the first person we recruited, in fact. We knew how desperate she was to change the image the public had of her, and she was the easiest to convince."

"I can imagine that," nodded Eric. "For many people, that scene with the little girl was what really launched the show. On numerous polls, it's come top as people's most dramatic moment so far. Did you always know that would be a pivotal scene? Why do you think it resonated so much with viewers?"

"I thought it would be important," answered Selina. "But it was the actors themselves who have to take most of the credit. 'Frank' (I still call him that as he was so good) getting her to open up and believe all that fake terminology, Meryl starring as the co-pilot and of course Nina the little girl connecting with her in a short time, meant that viewers were feeling all these different emotions at the same time. So, when the big moment came, it was even better than we'd hoped."

"I have to ask. Did you think she would give up her parachute?"

"I did, yes," said Selina without hesitating. "I was as shocked as everyone else. You saw the betting figures."

"Why do you think she didn't?" probed Eric.

"She valued her life above everyone else's. Her words and actions were very different. She was told a six-year-old girl was finally in remission, having spent her whole life in hospital, and still thought, no, me first."

"What do you think happens to Linda now?"

"That's up to her," replied Selina in the cold tone her contestants knew well. "My involvement with her ended when she left the studio."

"You haven't reached out?" responded Eric, surprised.

"Her game's over, and we move on. The referee wouldn't follow a player into the dressing room. Especially when the game is still going."

"Very much still going," smiled Eric. "The second challenge created an even stronger controversy. First off, the clowns all carried a baseball bat. Numerous charities said it glorified violence."

"It didn't glorify anything."

"You don't think you could have made the point with just the clowns?"

"And why not have *The Godfather* with water pistols instead of guns and *The Karate Kid* without any martial arts?" joked the TV head. "We ramped up the drama. That's been our philosophy all along. It comes back to my point earlier. We are an all caps and exclamation points, shackles off kind of show. We don't believe in bowling-lane bumpers or training-wheel bikes."

"But *The Godfather* and The *Karate Kid* franchises are fiction."

"It's not fiction; it's entertainment. It all comes under the same umbrella."

"Weren't you worried that it would have led to a heart attack? Jed Dexter is 52. Studies show that above 50, the chance of a heart attack in males increases substantially."

"We had him tested before the competition and had metal chips fitted throughout the task to ensure he wasn't at risk. The problem with those medical studies is that they act like everyone over 50 is the same. Jed is in great shape for his age. I find it unhelpful and discriminatory to lump everyone as though they are the same just based on when they were born."

"The big question is this," said Eric with a long pause for dramatic effect. "Just what would have happened if he hadn't found the door in time?"

"Good question," said Selina as she sat back and her chair and laughed.

"And the answer to that question?"

"Honestly, an hour was plenty of time for him to have found it," said a slightly impatient Selina. "When we all tested it, the longest it took anyone was 22 minutes, and she had a limp. We had him down for 30 minutes tops."

"You still haven't answered it," insisted its slightly forceful host.

"He would have had to take on the clowns," answered Selina, quite surprised by this more determined side of her interviewer. "They were going to be staggered out, so it wasn't like we just set them all loose at the hour mark. And their feet were tied. Jed had all the advantages."

"How do you think Jed would have done against a clown? I know a lot of viewers said Jed could have just walked towards him and with the smell the clowns would all have just run off!"

"Quite! You never know how people will react. As he reminds us so often, Jed is in good shape for his age. He's right that he could pass for mid-forties. Once he'd been given some extra fluids, he was shoved in a shower and given new clothes. The people laughing at his malfunction are missing the point. He took on his greatest fear and passed. Sure, he needed extra time and a bit of luck, but he did complete it, and I think once the laughter dies down, people will have more respect for him."

"That's a valid point," nodded Eric. "But I'm curious. Were there no limits? If Jed hadn't found the door, he would have been there with clowns armed with baseball bats?"

"That was the game. Either he was going to win or the clowns were."

"The police are ok with this?" asked Eric with curiosity.

"They'd be ok with it when they saw the contract the contestants signed."

"I'd like to see that contract!"

"A lot of people want to see that contract," grinned Selina mischievously. "It doesn't mean they will."

"Well, if you change your mind, I'm adding myself to that list. There were rumours that you had changed the settings so as to make the exit easier for him to find."

"People love a good conspiracy theory! That would go against everything we believe in. Besides, the diagram was up during the Hot/Cold game on audio commentary, so if we'd just swapped a door or suddenly had a door appear, people definitely would have noticed."

"Why do you think he kept missing it?" pondered its amiable host.

"I don't know," responded Selina, genuinely bemused. "I'm still unsure why he kept ending up with the purple clown."

"It's my husband's favourite colour, hence Purple Reign Perceptions as the title of my husband's social media page. Yep, had to get some promotion in there. Let's move on to the third challenge. Denzel was one of the more popular contestants. Handsome, charming, build like a ripped fridge as quite a few commentators described him. I know a lot of people knew something about his sordid past. But I think more than a few of us were caught off guard by just how bad it was. How is he? The last we saw of him; he seemed to have lost his mind."

"The doctors are working on him," said Selina in a cold voice.

"You don't think you could have taken him sooner? It's gotten the most complaints from any challenge so far. Denzel's sister called it 'deplorable and upsetting.'"

"We recommend family members don't watch any challenges live. We made that clear to her and everyone else before the programme started. Some people can handle it. She very clearly couldn't. And it's not meant to be a holiday camp. We could have pulled him out after 10 seconds. It wouldn't have been much of a challenge. Or fun to watch. And we wouldn't have learnt anything."

"Was the challenge different to how you thought it would end up?"

"Honestly, we never know. Obviously, we plan a lot of things. Removing the ring, the coffin microphones, the mention of spiders to throw him off, the sleeping gas to get him in there, etc. But that's the beauty of the show. We don't know what to expect, so viewers won't, either."

"Removing the ring was very devious," said Eric, half in admiration, half appalled.

"It was at the heart of the task, really. Stripping Denzel away from his football days to see what was left. The Super Bowl win was a big part of his identity. The mourner running late idea came from one of the team. Once we heard it, we had to sneak it in."

"What did you think of his speech at the end? He did seem contrite."

"It was quite moving. That's what the critics don't get. If we'd cut it earlier, we wouldn't have got that speech. Denzel really believed that was the end. You can't say you're going to push someone to the limit and then end the race as soon as the athlete starts to run out of breath. You'd miss out on all the drama at the end. There was an article released yesterday saying this is purely a revenge show. It's nothing of the sort."

"The Haskell Flinter piece in *The Independent Times*?" responded Eric immediately, though he checked his notes just to confirm.

"That's the one. I had several issues with what he wrote. Sponsors aren't falling out. None have quit. In fact, we've added two new ones since the last challenge. We've had to hire more staff on the merchandising team, and yesterday, we recruited several new members on the social media side who are fluent in different languages. No one on the team has left since we began."

"That's pretty emphatic."

"I'd also add that he was the one who said *Cobra Kai* would flop and *Orange Is the New Black* wouldn't last a season. I also read his original piece on *Breaking Bad* before he removed it and rewrote it once he realised how popular it was. Not to mention his *Ten Shows to Watch* last year featured seven that failed to get a renewal for a second series. Looking at it that way, I'm happy he's not a fan."

"Speaking of fans, it's time for the readers' questions now," said Eric as he went to a set of papers on his desk. "As you can imagine, we got a lot of people writing in. A few were outraged with the show's concept, but the majority were people saying how addicted they were and how they couldn't wait for the next two challenges."

"That's great to hear," said a genuinely happy Selina.

"Jefferson from Atlanta asks: Why don't you want to be on camera? Do you plan to make an appearance on the show at some point?"

"I've never been interested in being on TV," said Selina, puzzled as to why anyone would want to. "I'm more than happy being behind the scenes." She noticed Eric waving a paper of paper in front of her. "No, I can't see myself making an appearance," said Selina firmly, answering the question Eric had scribbled down. "The show is not about me, so why should I be on it?"

"Following on from that, have you been recognised?"

"No, I don't think my voice is that distinctive."

"Well, I wouldn't be surprised if it happens for you soon. Rockgod79 asks: Why are the challenges not fixed to a certain time? Is it to keep up the mystery?"

"That's a big part of it for sure. The fact you can be on your phone and suddenly, you have an hour to get ready to watch it is a big thrill. But it also takes a lot of planning. Remember that we never know which of the contestants it's going to land on, so each challenge has to be ready at the same time."

"That connects to a question Matilda de Waat from Rotterdam has. One that I meant to ask you earlier. How can you ensure that the wheel is 100% fair?"

"We have so much security guarding that wheel you'd think the President was in town. The room is also filmed with 24-hour security, and we have technicians check it before each show. I'd also add there's no need for us to interfere with it. It honestly wouldn't make any sense. This isn't a show where different people are paid different amounts to appear."

"And this is from England." Eric was about to attempt an accent but thought better of it. "Not really a question but he's definitely a fan. Alfie from Sheffield says: Love, love, love the show. Please tell us some trivia from behind the scenes, so I can impress the guys at work."

"Hi Alfie in Sheffield," beamed Selina, with the biggest smile since she'd sat down in the chair. "Well, Buck was our first and only choice for the role of host. We needed someone with charisma, energy and humour. He has his own designer, and before you ask, yes, he will be keeping the suits after the show."

"Oh, come on, you can give Alfie more than that!"

"Ok, have some extra," said Selina, with a wide grin. "He did say love three times after all! I was the first person to read the proposal. The show was at that point called *Wheel of Unfortunate*. There was always meant to be six contestants. They were the only six we asked. Due to specifically designed technology, the crowd can hear the contestants, but the contestants can't hear any specific words."

"You've got to be pleased with that, Alfie. FlyPinkSquirrel from Ontario, and quite a lot asked this question too, wants to know how you can fund such a big cash prize and such intricately planned challenges?"

"We have numerous sources. We have private benefactors, TV and promotional sponsorship, betting, merchandise, paid promotion and various subscriber premiums."

"Which has been the most significant?"

"We don't view things as singular, but as the collective. Some, like advertising and paid promotion, are paid in advance, while things like merchandising and betting change on a daily basis. What I would say is that through the weeks, all arrows have been going up. We're thrilled with all the numbers."

"Durban Delight noted that the third challenge was Attack of the Clowns but wants to know what the first two were called."

"A very astute question," said an admiring Selina. "The first was called Ascent into Madness and the second was Coffin up Secrets. It was mentioned in both of the commentaries, but I'll make sure each challenge's title is shown on the regular programme from now on."

"Of course, coffing without the G," smiled Eric. "A big one to finish with. SuziePikachu wants to know if you have any phobias?"

"No, I don't have any phobias."

"Would you tell us if you had?"

"Probably not," Selina laughed slyly. "But honestly, I don't. I've always faced my fears, anyhow. I didn't like heights, but that wasn't going to stop me paragliding when I visited South America and had the chance to try it when I was in Gemelas, Argentina. It's gorgeous, especially when looking down on it from the sky."

"Did I read you were afraid of water, too, even though you were a swimming champion?"

"You have done your research!" said the TV executive, genuinely impressed. "That's why my mother made me take it up and why I felt so driven to become a swimming champion before I gave it up at 16. Fear will never hold me back."

"So you'd have gone on the show?"

"If I was in the same place as the contestants, sure. I've always been a fighter."

"Anything else you'd like to add to all the followers of the shows listening to this?

"Keep watching. There's plenty more surprises left."

"Well, that's all we have time for today. Thank you to former swimming champion Selina Stevenson for her time answering questions. Water nice time I hope you've had on the show. She might have felt thrown in at the deep end, but she was far from all at sea, and I think it went swimmingly. I hope she continues to pool her talents with others on the show. And that's it from me. Thanks for listening to the best Cho around."

And with that, it was done.

IV

Madison, Yasmeen and Nate didn't hear the interview, but they were among the precious few who had no idea what was said. Different quotes were taken from the show. Some focused on the attack on Laronda Johnson, something the actress didn't take lying down. She launched back with heightened emotion, a lack of facts and repetitive logic, spewing that Selina was a "desperate wannabe who was just too cowardly to be on TV", "knew nothing about anything" and "winning a few trophies doesn't mean you can tell me what to do". When media sources conveniently linked details about Johnson's failed projects, plus diva-live behaviour to low-level staffers, things went quiet.

Other outlets focused more on the mysterious contract, how the show was being funded, how the six were the only ones considered and how Selina herself said she wouldn't go on the show. Haskell wrote a rebuttal piece but was laughed out of town after his original *Breaking Bad* review was mysteriously leaked. Opposition referenced in her interview tried to defend themselves but were being listened to less and were continually savaged in the comments section within each piece.

The three contestants continued as before, but there was no hiding that things were dull. Denzel's removal, while fantastically dramatic, left a big hole. The energy and romantic tension had evaporated from the room, and it was clear a sullen Yasmeen or a contemplative Madison were of no use. Nate had tried out some of his newest routines, but no one had the heart to humour him. Something that was abundantly clear when a hungry Yasmeen refused to wait for the punchline while waiting for her toast and left Nate talking to himself.

Something had to give, and Selina wasn't the type to hang around. Without even consulting others within the team, she decided to act.

Nate cursed as the power went when he was in the middle of unlocking a new level in his Fortnite game, having felt it was time for newer challenges. Yasmeen muttered "typical" as the light went off in her room and she was unable to finish reading. Madison didn't even notice initially, as she was in the guys' room, listening to music in the dark and still wondering what was going on in the outside world. Pausing the music, she could tell by the other two's frustrated yells that the electricity had gone. Fitting metaphor about trying to find light in a dark place, she mused.

Wanting to see if the lights had gone off everywhere, the three met, confused, in the hallway. It was the first time all three had been together since walking in after the last spin. "Fancy seeing you here," said Nate with a sarcastic grin.

Madison moved to the kitchen. "I'm sure I saw a box of matches somewhere," she said distractedly, as she rummaged around in some nearby draws. She would have been looking a long time. On the second night, Jed had accidentally knocked them in cream and had thrown them all away without telling anyone.

"Our apologies for the technical difficulties," came out Selina's voice from the loudspeakers. "We are working hard to fix everything."

Nate went to the freezer and took out ice cream.

"I'll have some, too, thanks," called out Madison. She was impressed with Nate's dexterity in the dark, who grinned.

"I've been there enough times, I could do it blindfolded," said Nate with a chuckle.

"If anyone asks, I'm having extra because you know, with the power out, the ice cream will melt," said Madison, and laughed for the first time since arriving back after the last challenge.

"Ah, reminds me of a time when I was on stage and this guy in the front row was eating this ice lolly and..."

Annoyed that Nate didn't even think to reach for her vegan ice cream, Yasmeen sulked and decided to go back to her room.

"You know, Yasmeen," began Madison. "You don't have to go ba..."

But Yasmeen was gone, stumbling and swearing on her way back, as she kept bumping into walls and tripping over the carpet.

"She doesn't like me, does she?" said Nate rather abruptly, after watching her leave.

Caught off guard, Madison found herself stuttering. "I wouldn't say... er, I mean... er...

"It's ok, I know she doesn't," said Nate resignedly.

"You don't exactly share culinary tastes or a similar lifestyle," reasoned Madison.

"I know! My dad told me never to trust someone who couldn't enjoy a cheeseburger."

Madison smiled before her look turned more solemn. "She didn't come here to make friends, none of us did. There's enough going on here. We're either walking out of here a winner or a loser. No middle ground."

"Nice try, but I saw the way you looked at Denzel when he was being dragged away. That was more than a stranger," said Nate, looking Madison right in the eye so she couldn't avoid the question.

"And look how that turned out!"

"Hang on, did I interrupt you guys on the couch...? That night..."

Madison sighed. "Don't worry about it. You actually saved me from something very stupid. I clearly didn't know him at all."

"Come on, none of us are getting VIP passes into heaven," said Nate with a grin. "We wouldn't be here if we were saints."

Nate put the ice cream down and looked at her directly. "Honesty time! What do you know about me?"

"You have a cute dog," said Madison. "You like basketball a lot and you're the most relaxed of any of us when the wheel is spinning. I wish I could be that calm."

"That's it?"

"Well, Denzel and Jed were always complaining you were a slob who was allergic to folded clothes and had no idea how to use coat hangers or trashcans."

"Don't tell me you're one of those girls who think folded clothes are sexy!" laughed Nate. "Anyhow, I meant from before this whole process."

"No, but don't take it personally," explained Madison with sincerity. "I wasn't interested in celebrities. I was in a bubble, desperate to prove myself in the family business and in other ventures. I wasn't exactly focused on the world around me and what they were up to, despite what the press seemed to think. I didn't date my exes because they were famous. They just happened to understand my lifestyle more. And now, I'm in a different kind of goldfish bowl. Funny how life works out."

"Nah, that's showbiz!" said an excitable Nate. "I know how hard I had to work to make it. The number of gigs, the rotten pay, other comics stealing my act. You don't forget those days. Trust me, a life without showbiz is even worse!"

"So what are you in here for?" said Madison, pausing beforehand as she deliberated whether the question was too personal.

Before Nate had a chance to answer, Yasmeen came along, holding two candles. "Let there be light," she said, beaming, and though Madison was annoyed by the interruption, she was happy to be out of the darkness.

"I finally found my lighter!" exclaimed Yasmeen. "Haven't smoked in years but never got rid of it. The bedroom is worse than a nuclear site trying to find it, but it was worth it. I thought I should share it with you guys."

She threw a sweatshirt that she'd been carrying on her shoulders at Nate. "I walked past your room and saw this lying on your bed. Figured you might need it."

"That's nice of you, thanks," said Nate, genuinely touched.

"So what were you guys talking about when I came in?" she asked inquisitively.

"Just about this process, really," answered Madison in a pensive fashion. "What it must be like to watch this as an outsider. How little we really know ourselves and each other. I was wondering if people would like us."

"I don't really care if they like me or not," said Yasmeen. "I don't live life to be popular. I just live it as me. If that's not enough for people, stuff them."

"So, why are you here?" asked Madison.

"Because I can reach people. The people like me who didn't quite fit in at school, who didn't grow up with that close circle of friends or weren't quite what their parents wanted or expected. I know the calming benefits of Pilates, of meditation. I know what life is like without that calming influence. I can reach out to those people."

"Did you do that before?" questioned Madison, surprised Yasmeen seemed so engaged for once.

"Very much so, but I made very bad mistakes," answered Yasmeen. "Then for a while, I just stayed in bed. Didn't eat or leave my room. But that's not who I am."

"You weren't tricked into this?" said an astonished Nate. "You've been like a bat out of hell since we got here."

"I wasn't chosen randomly off the street," fired back Yasmeen, keen to show she wasn't naïve. "I knew there would be sacrifices. I miss my long walks, my routine, my communication with my parents and sister. My tattoo artist, my massages, my local bakery. I hate being trapped in here like a caged animal."

"So what were you expecting?" said Madison, keen to find out more. "It was never going to be like my father's country club. All saunas and golf courses and grand ballrooms."

"It's not about what you expect," said Yasmeen emphatically. "It's about what you're prepared to do once you're here."

"So you want to win?"

"For sure," responded Yasmeen, surprised she was even being asked. "Just because I don't pump my chest out like Denzel or use fancy words like Jed doesn't mean I haven't taken this seriously. I already know what I would do with the money."

Nate had been about to make a joke about spending it all on vegan burgers, but he stopped himself in time. "What would you spend it on?" he asked more neutrally.

"I have big plans. I want to expand the business. Get more followers, more instructors, more awareness. I want to change people's mindsets about healthy living and veganism. There's still so much ignorance. It's helped me so much. I know it's not embraced by everyone yet, but with that money, I know I can reach out and increase knowledge and understanding."

Nate had wondered what he wanted to spend his money on, but no matter how he thought about it, he still couldn't better the idea Selina had suggested at the start. No matter what was going on in his life, the Knicks had always been there. Whether his grades were poor, his parents were arguing, or he struggled to get a girl to go out with him, the Knicks were right with him. He could still remember the way his father's face lit up when talking about the 1970 and 1973 wins. And if he really wanted to get his father talking, he'd just mention Willis Reed and game 7.

Madison never talked finances, so she thought it best not to add anything. She'd learnt the hard way that people without money never sympathised with people who had it, no matter how legitimate the grievances were.

There was a quiet for a few moments, with Nate in particular looking in deep thought. Suddenly, he asked, "Do you want any of your ice cream...Yasmeen?"

Madison was just as surprised as Yasmeen was, both glancing up at him in shock. Taking that as a yes, he went to grab some, using the candle to make sure he had the right kind.

Yasmeen smiled as she ate, perhaps the first time she had seemed content since the process began.

Wanting to avoid a sentimental moment, Nate thought it best to change the topic.

"Something I've been curious about. What did you think of the Taylor Swift wannabe?"

"I just wish she brought more positive energy," said Yasmeen, unaware of the amused looks Nate and Madison shared between them at Yasmeen's apparent lack of irony. "She had a closed mind to anything other than music. She had no interest in travel, or art, or literature. Dull girl, but I wish her well."

"Let's hope so," replied Nate, with a tilt of the head. "Watching her bundled out of the studio reminded me of what those virgins must have looked like just before they were chucked into a volcano." And without sentiment, he grabbed himself a beer, checking the others already had a drink.

"I gave up trying to be liked in high school," continued Nate as he opened his can. "Just hang out with people who can make you laugh is my philosophy. If they like basketball and video games, that's a bonus."

"I was taught in a private school and very much taught to be a lady," said Madison, rolling her eyes. "I mean, what the hell does that even mean, anyhow?" She kicked off one of her heels and threw it to the other end of the room.

Yasmeen looked on in approval at this sudden show of rebellion.

"That might be the biggest surprise since I got here," said Yasmeen with a smile. "Welcome to the dark side."

"I'm not the prim princess you seem to think I am. I'm no goody two shoes."

The others looked at her in interest. "Are you sure?" questioned a disbelieving Nate. "I mean, I figured you as the sophisticated, classy wildcard, chosen to make the rest of us look worse."

"I've made mistakes, just as you have," responded a defensive Madison.

"Oh, do tell," said Yasmeen, with a mischievous smile.

"There's no point going into that now," said the heiress, resigned. "It will all come out soon enough," She raised her glass of wine, as she prepared for a toast. "To Linda, Jed and Denzel. See you guys on the other side."

And with that, she went to her bed and prepared to sleep, the exhaustion and alcohol seemingly hitting at the same time. "Lightweight," shouted Nate after her, but he was pretty tired himself. He looked at Yasmeen and she looked back at him, both feeling a little uncertain how to act now their buffer had gone.

"I'd better go," Yasmeen said awkwardly. "I have a feeling she'll fall asleep on the wrong bed." Nate chuckled and went back to his room.

Selina watched this all with interest. She had wanted some honesty, and she was happy with how it turned out. Despite what she told the contestants, it wasn't live. There was a one-minute loop just in case any of the group broke rank and said something that couldn't be broadcast. She was fine with swearing, even though some of their better-paying advertisers frowned upon it. Thankfully, the three had avoided anything slanderous or anything that painted the competition in too negative a light. The show had been missing a sense of connection.

When the three awoke at different parts of the day the morning after, it was with a whole different set of emotions. Nate woke up trying to guess what day it was. He had a feeling the Knicks would be playing today, and he missed his chats with his friends about the team's chances. If they won this match, they'd be in with a great shout for the playoffs.

Yasmeen got up, desperate for some juice. She noticed with a smile that the pile of leaflets she had left on veganism had been moved to the couch, with some left open. The crumbs would have been enough of a cue, even without the conversation the night before. She wondered whether to say anything to Nate, but the guys' room was locked, and she knew better than to disturb him.

Very little happened afterwards. After the more in-depth chat two nights ago, the three had been enjoying the calmer day, having all felt they all revealed a little too much. Yasmeen was able to get back to her artwork and Spanish, while Nate ignored the video games and TV so as to focus on his writing. Madison did some light gym work and diary writing, but really had spent most of the day asleep, something Selina worried viewers at home would be doing, if not changing the channel.

If there was one thing Selina hated, it was boredom. She'd hoped things would have developed from the previous night's conversation, but that had obviously passed. She'd wondered about deliberately flooding the men's room due to a technical leak or rat infestation, but she thought better of it. Once the contestants realised they could be manipulated, it was over. Instead, she focused on getting everything ready for the fourth challenge.

As the lightest sleeper of the three, Nate was woken up first by the klaxon. He thought he might be dreaming. He certainly had a history of wacky dreams, helped by his love of watching horror films before going to bed. But he soon realised it was real when he could hear the loud swearing of Yasmeen even from the other end of the flat.

Instinctively, he looked to see what time it was, but even without a clock, he knew it would be the early hours. He'd watched enough reality shows to learn they always needed to keep some cards up their sleeve. He showered and had some cereal, before watching some comedy to put him in a more relaxed mood.

Yasmeen got up angrily, cursing to herself as she had a long shower. As she got dressed, she realised she couldn't be this angry while in the studio. She had to calm down. She had no idea how people without meditation and Pilates coped.

Madison stayed in bed until she heard the security team. Rather than the polished, well-groomed lady she liked to present herself as, she was dragged out of bed by two staff with her hair unkempt and in her nightie. The usually stylish blonde only just had time to grab a dressing gown but was unable to put on some shoes or throw her stuff on the bed like the others had.

So it was quite the trio that walked into the studio. A bandanna-wearing Nate with a t-shirt that said "Nate Reeder, Non-Reader". An outwardly calm but inwardly seething Yasmeen who loathed losing out on sleep. And Madison, who looked everything she was. A heavy sleeper who had been dragged from her bed, hair all over the place, no make-up and with her sexy nightwear only hidden by a robe.

It may have been 6 am local time, but Buck was still full of energy, bouncing around on stage, wearing a sparkling blue suit and still with that dazzling smile. Madison wondered if he ever slept.

"It may be early people, but it's never too early for another spin of the wheel. I'm ready! Are you ready?" he roared, beckoning the crowd to respond. As always, they responded to his infectious joy with unbridled passion, standing up from their seats, pumping their fists and shouting how much they loved him.

"We started off with six, now we're halfway down. Each of the three players has a 33.3% chance of winning and twice as much chance of going home. We're going to be finding out who they are very soon. Before we spin that wheel for the penultimate time, let's see how they're doing."

He immediately went to ask a question of Madison, but seeing how exhausted she was, decided to come back to her later.

"Nate," said Buck, putting his arm around him. "We're at the halfway point. You've seen three people go. How are you feeling?"

"Ah, you know, life's just a game. We're just adding some drama and some style to it." He then looked at Buck, adding, "Not to mention comedy."

"I've gotta say, you have quite the fan club. I'm going to read out some quotes from viewers. "Is Nate single? Which comedians does he most admire? Is mayo ever acceptable on a hot dog?

"Single, yeah. Please pass that on to Dua Lipa. I am the most attractive male contestant left, after all, so that has to help my chances. My absolute favourite comedians are George Carlin and Richard Prior. Legends that pushed the boundaries and left us far too soon. Finally, no, mayo is never acceptable on a hot dog. Honestly, people, if you see someone eating a hot dog with mayo, you should be looking for the nearest bin. For the hot dog, or the person, whichever is easiest."

Buck did some flamboyant and energetic rhythmic moves before looking at Yasmeen, who was unimpressed.

"Tough crowd today, people, I tell you," said Buck with a grin. "Okay, no dancing. But I'm curious to know which has been your favourite and your least favourite moment here." "Hmmmm," said Yasmeen with a contemplative look. "My favourite moment has been the times with my artwork. That's easy. I've really challenged myself to try more ambitious drawings. I'm in a good place creatively. Worst. Well, there are several. Realising there was no garden, no clock, no individual room. Living with someone who is able to get six different types of meat on a pizza. All the uncertainty of these spins. And let's be honest. Now isn't great. I'm not really a morning person."

"A reminder, people, that this is not an audience vote," deadpanned the infectious host, to raucous laughter.

"Speaking of non-morning people, here's Madison. I say this with love, but did you sleep in a hedge last night?"

"It certainly wasn't the Egyptian cotton I do normally," she said with an attempted grin, but without the right delivery, she took the atmosphere out of the room.

"Don't worry, we wouldn't mistake you for a peasant." He rolled his eyes in slight contempt but still evoked a ripple of laughter from the audience. "She's just like you and me, except that her father could probably buy France if he wanted to."

Madison wanted to try and fix things, but Buck wasn't going to let her have it. If you didn't have a quip within a split second, you were gone.

"I'll keep it to one short question," said Buck. "If you could have brought one family member or friend to come into the process with you, who would you have chosen?

"That's a good question. I mean, I'm not sure my parents would do well in this situation. My brother Harvey is too competitive. He wouldn't be able to deal with the waiting around and sense of luck. My younger brother Vincent would probably annoy the others too much. He's great, but pretty chatty. My best friend Veronica would make me laugh, but she does like her fixed routine. I guess..."

"I'm glad I didn't ask you three questions," said Buck, as he fell to his knees with laughter. "The decisive Madison Larouch, everybody."

"What time is it?" asked Madison with eyes squinted.

"Time for a new spin," replied Buck with total smoothness and the maximum of energy. "We're down to three. And in a few moments, we will find out who is next to leave and take on the challenge of doom."

It was interesting because, for the first time, the betting was more or less equal.

Nate was 34.2%, Madison was 33.5% and Yasmeen was 32.3%.

The three then each chose a ball, Nate energetically, Yasmeen disinterestedly and Madison distractedly. That then led to the random allocation, ending with:

Nate Reeder: Green 4
Madison Larouch: Yellow 5
Yasmeen Kahley: White 6

"It's all in the wheel, how do you feel? Your lucky day or are you on your way?" he chanted as he gave the wheel a big push.

With only three names left, it seemed like every time one of the three blinked, they could see their name flash by again. Nate was the only one who could bear to look. Yasmeen instead focused on the crowd, picking out different faces and wondering what their backstory was. Why were people so fascinated by this show? Madison stared down at the floor, then, remembering her family name, stood up straight. She could tell that the wheel was slowing down as she could feel the suspense just by the audience's sounds.

The others felt it, too, with the three now focused on where it was going to land. Nate was reminded of a quote he'd heard when watching a replay of the Knicks landing a crucial shot against the Pistons. "Strange how in slow motion, the ball seemed to hang in the air for even longer."

He hadn't thought of that line in years, and now it came to him and seemed perfect.

The smile was wiped off his face when the wheel finished on his name. Nate stared at it. His name in big letters on the green background. The first time the audience had guessed right, and now it was him. He actually started to laugh, much to the astonishment of Madison and Yasmeen.

"You do know what his means for you?" Madison asked, trying to be caring but unintentionally coming off as patronising.

"At least you're out of here," said Yasmeen, having to speak louder than she intended due to all the background noise.

"Nate, Nate, Nate," said Buck sadly. "I'm gonna miss you and your t-shirts." He grabbed him in a hug. The audience responded warmly.

"Well, the audience finally got it right! Only just, mind, but correct. This is why you need to keep going, because you can keep getting it right and win big. Nate, that won't be you. Gotta say, my man, you're taking it better than some others have here. What do you want to say to the people here and out there?"

"It's been a hell of a ride," he said with a rueful grin. "For me, it's the hardest gameshow, but I'm glad I signed up. I got a chance to meet some new people, put myself into a new environment and give myself a chance to win big. That's what life is all about. Now, if you could just find a technical fault which means the spin has to be replayed..."

"Funny to the end," said Buck with feeling. Nate grabbed a hug from Madison and Yasmeen and then waved to the audience as he was escorted towards the exit as his video started to play.

"I'm Nate Reeder. Only my parents called me Nathan. So, if I hear that then it's either my parents came back to life, miss you both, or there's a big twist in the family history. Or you know, you're like a butler. Though I think butlers would put a Mr in front of things. Or is it Master? I'd love a butler. Funny to think something so posh starts with a butt!

"Anyhow, yeah, I'm a comedian. I won my Best Newcomer award when I was just 23, the youngest since it was launched in 1977. It looked like a dog had been squished by a car, which was cool because my winning routine was all about how life would be if a dog became president. That was validation for everything I'd done. I was never one for school. I did all kinds of rotten jobs for a while until I made it. I had to work every kind of job until the 'Komedy Klinic' finally let me have a slot after a late cancellation. After that night, things changed for me. I was like an overnight success, getting a big agent and being booked for venues. And when I went on the Danny Lemont chat show, it blew up even more. Funny how you can bomb on stage, but exploding onto the scene means the complete opposite."

Nate noticed the question of "Why are you here?" before he had finished laughing at his last joke. "I guess it's time to get serious." His expression changed as suddenly as though day turned to night.

"I'm here because I messed up," he said sadly. "I just like to make people laugh. I want people to laugh so much they fall off their chair or have to stop driving. That's what I live for. The ultimate drug. And I know I've got it wrong sometimes. I know that joke about the football stadium tragedy was too much too soon, and about that kidnapped girl on the news. I thought she was older than 13. I wanted to remind people that I made the joke before they found the body and we all found out they'd done stuff even after she was dead. As I said at the time, I am sorry about that one. I'm not just saying that because all my gigs and panel shows were cancelled. That wasn't a joke I had written beforehand. It just came out as part of my act, and I regret it."

There was a long gap as Nate avoided looking at the camera. "I know after those jokes, a lot of newspapers did some digging, and it was open season for me. I know I wasn't always a great boyfriend or a great friend. I will do better. And that begins with this show. I want to use my humour for good. I was down for a while, but I will go in there with a smile."

Nate was thinking about that video while he was put into the car and in a direction in which he had no idea where it was heading. Part of it was to ensure he wouldn't be thinking about his challenge, but he knew he had made a lot of mistakes. It's quite something to hear all your worst moments read back to you in front of strangers and two people who he had started to bond with.

Having seen Madison's reaction when Denzel's self-confessed social rap sheet was read out, he knew better than to have looked at either of them during his video. He wondered if they would ever chat again on the outside, but he knew in his heart what would happen. They'd walk right past or else make some vague suggestion about meeting up but with no intention of doing so. Outside of his beloved Knicks, he was a realist. He knew the pair would be doing their best to forget their time there. And that was before whatever aftermath they'd be dealing with the aftermath of their challenges.

He may have been stupid once, but that was a while ago. And it was understandable. Taking years to make it, having to take all kinds of menial jobs while his parents questioned his sanity, abilities and ambition, why shouldn't he enjoy it? The sold-out performances, the adulation from critics and fans, all the perks from free stuff, VIP access and elite parties. There were nowhere near as many groupies as he'd dreamed about, but he couldn't complain. It was a great life.

The main problem had been trying to get acceptance from the comedians he had grown up respecting. When he won his award and started becoming a celebrated name, they refused to give him any acknowledgement or recognition. And so, it was like high school, doing things he wouldn't otherwise have done to get more credibility from the cool kids. And just like in high school, it all ended badly, for him as well as his victims.

So yeah, he had to take some blame. But then, he had all these experts. What was the point of them? They had all these fancy qualifications, but they had still not warned him about how certain news stories were best avoided. Sports stars were given regular media training. Why wasn't he? Not to mention his big-time agent. For someone to screw up, it had to be more than one person's fault. When a famous pal of his wrote a funny but badly received column about a child star's battle with drug addiction, no one blamed the editor for not spotting how badly it would be received. They just went for the big name. Being a celebrity was an easy target. That's something people never considered.

He wished he could have learnt more useful things during his time at school. Less about how to play the recorder or the difference between sedimentary and igneous rocks and more about being able to read a room. Who knew what his former teachers were thinking? Maybe they were even watching the show. They benefited then and they'd be benefitting again.

Of course, there was still that challenge. A thought that came more to prominence when the car stopped. Getting out, he realised he was in an isolated area, with decaying buildings and no hint of anything green. Nate may not have known where he was, but he recognised the kind of place this was. It wasn't poor, there wasn't any crime, but it was just bland. No one around him had any real ambition, but he had been determined to get out of there and make something of himself. And before his fall from grace, he had.

The Queens native wished he was wearing more than a t-shirt and jeans. For the first time since he'd come into the process, he felt cold. The 31-year-old shivered as he looked around at the stench of poverty, with the horrible feeling he was being watched. It's a feeling he should be used to. Since he'd entered the show, he'd been like a circus freak show. It was just made worse now as he was closer to the audience.

Suddenly, a phone was handed to him with a voice on the line he recognised very well.

"Hello, Nate," said Selina in the business-like tone she was known for. "As your name came up in the wheel, you know it's time for your challenge. Please follow the security team out of the car and into the room before you will be given further instructions."

Before Nate could say anything, he was bundled into a small, empty room in the nearest building. There was only one chair. No table, no window, not even a carpet. And definitely no clock. All he could do was sit and think about how he was going to have no money after all his effort and a very unpleasant challenge was coming up. But how bad was it going to be?

After a while, he was given a blindfold and earmuffs and taken up a staircase by those burly security guards. Honestly, they were bigger than a Mount Rushmore carving. It was a lot of stairs. He was tired and sweaty, so one of them just picked him up and carried him as though he was a bottle of ketchup. Finally, after what seemed like an eternity, a door was pushed, and he was let down.

Once his earmuffs and blindfold were removed, he realised how bad things were. He'd never liked heights, and he was definitely way above ground level. At least 30 blocks' worth. He went to open the door, but it was locked solid. There was no way even any of the primates who carried him up would be able to knock it down. The only way out was using the two ropes going from this building to the other, about 30 feet across. It wasn't quite a tightrope though, as there was a rope at chest height to hold onto either side.

Voices from different windows were looking out at him, calling out things, but he couldn't focus on anything enough to hear it. What he could hear was a loudspeaker and something being read as though from a screen. "My grandmother is funnier than this loser, and she's been dead five years". There was a moment's gap before another voice read out a different message. "Nate is useless, as boring as he is stupid. As funny as his face."

Nate actually grinned. If this was part of the torture, he could deal with it fine. Being a comedian, he'd heard far worse. The 31-year-old even quoted some in his act. He went to inspect the upper rope, wondering how strong it was. Nate had never been slim or athletic. The idea of a rope from one building to put his feet on and only one rope to hold on to was terrifying, but he could do it. As long as he concentrated, and did it slowly, he could do it. He sighed. As unpleasant and dangerous as this was, he thought it was worse. Luckily, Selina hadn't discovered his ultimate phobia.

Suddenly, there were mechanical noises from below, but what got his attention was a drone. By the close level of control, it was obviously being operated by a true expert. He was also aware it was carrying something. But what most got his attention was the huge container underneath the bridge. He'd seen the machines below but assumed that was just the camera crew. But the large metal container was being moved with great precision underneath the ropes in order to fit exactly underneath the rope bridge. If only he could see inside.

The drone was flying closer and closer, seemingly in sync with the machines below. They sure were working fast. The container was now exactly underneath the ropes and between both buildings. He could hear something being dropped by the drone behind him, but he couldn't take his eyes off the container. Though the impatient kid in him was desperate to read the note, he got an ominous feeling about the huge container and found it impossible to look away.

With great noise from the forklift trucks, and hushed sounds from the crowd, it was getting closer to the big reveal. Finally, after a further measurement check, the forklift trucks moved away.

Nate wasn't close enough to see their faces, but he could hear them. Baying for blood, wanting as much drama as possible. He felt like one of those Roman slaves waiting for the unlocked lion to emerge into the arena. And in those cases, it tended to go better for the lion.

With three short whistles and plenty of cheering, the metal container's final outer laying was removed to all kinds of breathless anticipation. And it was worse than Nate could imagine.

He immediately saw what it was and recoiled.

Snakes. Hundreds and thousands of snakes. Where one began and one ended was impossible to tell. It was just one big blur of horrendous colours slithering around, with the added disgust of that vile hissing noise. He covered his ears, but the reptiles seemed just as loud no matter what direction they moved in. The idea of him being in that pit with them made his own skin crawl.

Nate had remained calm since entering the competition. He had been determined not to lose his composure and ruin all the effort he had made to seem a pleasant guy who had made one or two less-than-pleasant jokes. Unlike others in the process, he never forgot he was being filmed. Nor did he play an exaggerated or duller version of himself. Everything had been carefully managed.

But inside, he was screaming. He rubbed his eyes, desperate to wake up. And yet all he could see when he did open them was snakes. Even their sound was freaking him out. That hissing. He couldn't get it out of his head. He wanted to cover his eyes and his ears and yet he found himself powerless to do either.

He'd been afraid of them ever since he had gone camping as a ten-year-old and someone had thrown one in his tent as a prank, and he'd been bitten. It turned out the snake wasn't venomous, but he'd been scared of them, and scarred from the experience, ever since.

Seeing all those snakes brought back all that terror and all those nightmares he had had since. He cut those friends out of his life, never went camping again and never mentioned it to friends, family, exes or colleagues. Nothing in his act or in interviews. How the hell had she found out?

He staggered away from the bridge and found himself where the drone had dropped off the document. He slapped himself in order to compose himself and read the note entitled Viperchondria, a pun he would usually have found funny.

Dear Nate

To avoid falling into the container filled with non-venomous vipers below, you must get to the other side using the two ropes you see before you. It is the only way across. Remaining on this section without moving (or merely standing on the ropes without any effort to get across) will lead to increasing levels of punishment.

Selina had really done her homework. Nate knew if he had been watching at home, it was a show he would have watched with a bucket of popcorn and Zeus by his side.

But that didn't help him now. He had to focus. He'd lost out on the money, and the continued rehabilitation of his image, but he still had a part to play. He knew performers were judged by the end. Some gags landed better than others, but as long as you left them wanting more at the end, things were good.

So, he began to concentrate. Oddly, the insults had stopped. He wasn't sure when; he'd been so focused on trying to block the noise of those hideous creatures. He half-grinned despite himself, as he knew it must be because they had no effect on him. A rare mistake by Selina. Another expert overvalued.

He wasn't to know that the insults had always been a short appetiser. Five insults were randomly chosen by five lucky competition winners. Selina and her team had gone through a whole heap of message boards to find the ones to make the longlist. There really were all kinds of people out there, with all kinds of vocabulary. And not all lawyers would have found them as amusing as she and the team did.

Nate did not know how long he had been standing there without moving, but he got some idea when he heard the loudspeaker. "Official warning. You have to enter the bridge within five minutes, or the first added punishment will come into play."

If the snakes were bad enough when they were below him, the idea of one moving so fast so near to him made his skin crawl. It wasn't just him. Think about it, he said to himself. Even The Bible hates snakes. The snake wasn't exactly the good guy in *Harry Potter* or *The Jungle Book*. Movies and cartoons could make rats, spiders and sharks lovable. Snakes were beyond help.

But Nate had read enough sporting biographies to understand you have to respond to adversity. You don't get anything in life by feeling sorry for yourself.

So, he began to move towards what you could loosely call a bridge. Things would only get worse if he just stood there, so he slowly put one foot on the rope and tried to ignore all the disgusting sounds from below.

That's when things started to get interesting. For one, the ropes really weren't as sturdy as he had imagined. A little too much force, and he would fall down to the… that sentence wasn't worth finishing. He had told himself that no matter how loud the noise got from below, he would not look down. It was easier to focus on the cloudy skies. Nate never minded when it wasn't sunny. It meant he sweat less, and it was less noticeable when he wore baggy clothing.

But that wasn't the only problem. The loudspeaker was back. And it certainly got his attention. The shock of the name mentioned almost made him fall straight in.

"Felicity Terksbury was spotted at the Kileman Surgery today," read out a voice he recognised as the father of the woman he had dated for three years. "The 31-year-old TV actress and former girlfriend of comedian Nate Reeder did her best to disguise herself, but onlookers immediately recognised the former presenter of *Seaside Road* and star of numerous hit shows…"

The voice carried on with a little extra description, with speculation as to what cosmetic work she was getting done, but Nate did his best to zone out. The mere mention of her name, and hearing her disapproving father's voice, too, still freaked him out. Truth be told, he had treated her badly. She'd been an amazing actress, but always so insecure. It had been tiring. He wanted the confident, funny, sassy character she played to perfection in *Ravenous Sirens*, about a group of friends from high school who have to set up an elite escort business to qualify for a quirky inheritance. Instead, he got a woman who was always paranoid about whether she was the most attractive on the show. She needed so much reassurance all the time. It never made any sense to him. Nate was an out-of-shape guy with intense cravings for junk food and a hatred of the gym. And he wasn't bothered by what people thought of his appearance.

At first, it annoyed him, then he saw the comedic possibilities of her freak-outs. He hadn't intended to. It was just the odd joke here and there. But once he started, it was impossible to stop. The problem was, neither did she. He figured she'd eventually laugh it off. But with each surgery or procedure, she started becoming a freak show, and Nate couldn't even stand to look at her, let alone make any more animal references. Nor could anyone else. Her TV career soon plummeted, and she was forced to take on radio shows given to her by a sympathetic friend high up in the entertainment industry.

Nate had always prided himself on stopping the jokes as soon as they split. He was a gentleman, after all. But listening to the different articles, with dates and quotes from worried friends and colleagues, he realised he could have stopped the jokes far earlier and been more sympathetic. Her concerned family had tried to reach out before, but he was a master at looking serious and pretending to care while mentally checking out. It was a skill he'd mastered on all his menial jobs. But up on the flimsiest of bridges, knowing he was being judged it was different. He couldn't even cover his ears. That would just mean he would fall into the snakes below. He had nothing to do but listen. And for the first time, he felt ashamed of how he had treated her.

"You need to get moving," boomed a voice. "Merely holding onto the bridge without making any effort to move forwards is an offence and will not be tolerated."

What did that mean, not tolerated? wondered Nate. It wasn't like this was a holiday camp and he was enjoying himself stuck 30 feet above a pit of snakes. But realising he had been a jerk to someone who had since fallen on bad times wasn't going to get him out of this mess. He would have to keep moving. Besides, once he had moved, it was bound to be easier.

Wrong! Nate went to move one foot forward, but he wobbled. "Oh my God, the pressure's too much, and I'm going in!" screamed Nate. "The rope won't hold, it won't hold!" he exclaimed as Nate leaned too much to the right. Whether watching on TV, a computer screen or a portable device, viewers found themselves screaming, either instructions as to how he could stay up or to hurry up and fall in.

After some frantic leaning to the left, he was able to get back to a vertical position. Only just. His sweaty hands were finding it harder to grip, and Nate found he couldn't move. After the shock from before, he was paralysed with fear. All he could do was stand as still as possible and do everything to keep his balance. When his fingers got tired of the intense pressure of holding onto the rope, he would let it go for the briefest of seconds. And listen to more of his ex-girlfriend's descent into surgical suicide. He had no idea how long had passed until he heard the same voice as before.

"You were warned," said the voice, even angrier. He immediately heard noises below. Very cautiously, he glanced down and could see movement. It was the same guys who had installed the container. They weren't going to move it away, were they? Nate asked himself. There was no space to put more snakes in, either. So, what were they doing?

He soon found out. They weren't removing snakes, but they were adding an extra layer. In other words, they were going to increase the height of the snakes. He was going to see and hear them more than before. And he was guessing that if he didn't move along, the height would keep going up until it didn't matter if he fell in.

Adding the extra five feet did not take as long as he thought it would. Maybe because he was slow, everything else seemed faster. But he knew Selina operated things methodically. Her lame insults through the loudspeaker had been her only misstep. Now he thought about it, that power cut happened at a convenient moment. She was devious.

Well, he wasn't going to give them what they wanted. He knew how reality shows worked. They wanted tears. They wanted drama. They wanted him to fall into that pit of snakes. Crying, screaming, whatever. That wasn't going to be him.

All his life, he had been underestimated. Just because he didn't use fancy words, wear a smart suit or have a Captain America physique, people thought he was nothing special. But in gym class, he had climbed that rope when they were all ready to laugh at him. He had got that successful career when all his teachers thought he would spend his life stacking boxes. He'd landed himself hot girlfriends when all his friends thought he would have to accept the first woman who said yes.

Singing the lyrics to Eminem's "Lose Yourself", or some of them as he couldn't control his heavy breathing, Nate got going. He was going to do this. Yes, he was. More like a scared tortoise than a graceful monkey, but he was moving. He moved his right foot forward very gingerly, with as much care and precision as if he were walking in a minefield. Which, in effect, he was.

The ropes were so shaky. Nate knew that was the whole point. He knew the people all wanted drama. He had no idea what the other challenges had been, but this had to have been the worst. Two phobias in one, really.

But he was desperate to think about the positives. As long as he kept moving, and he kept upright, he'd be ok. The details about Felicity were distracting, but he vowed he would help her when he got out. Even if she or her family weren't receptive, he would try. The media would never find out. Not from him. There'd be no photos, but maybe his agent could helpfully let a few news agencies know. Kindness always means more when others can see it.

He'd been slow, but he knew he had made progress. He could tell by the noises of the crowd, even without his steps. Nate was starting to get their respect. They'd have seen his reaction to the snakes. It was a serious condition. Ophidiophobia. He remembered checking it up once. Sure, he couldn't be able to spell it drunk, or let's be honest, sober, but he could be a spokesperson. Maybe a role on TV where he got to talk to people affected by snakes. Or who were trying to protect them. Whatever worked best for ratings. Plenty of other comedians did serious TV work.

He was still moving slowly, but he counted five steps forward. He was about a third of the way through. He wasn't elegant but could start to see progress. He was even wondering what was on the other end of the bridge. Selina had said the challenge ended there. Surely, she wouldn't lie?

She couldn't lie, not on live TV. It was different lying in Poker or when playing basketball. Or even to a girlfriend. But lying when you could be proven to lie, and in front of others, now that was bad. He knew he would be fine. All he had to do was keep doing what he was doing.

He had found the trick was to move forward with a slight balance to the right, and then a slight lean to the left. Otherwise, there would be too much pressure, like before. He guessed people would be impressed. He knew they all wanted him to fall in. He had no idea how the other challenges had gone, but he knew this time they'd be unhappy. There was no way he was going in that pit.

The 31-year-old wanted to look at the crowd to show that he was something. He wanted to look back at the other end of the bridge to show how far he had managed. Like when you're in a long queue or looking back at a traffic jam. But he wasn't stupid. He could do all that when he had gotten off this rotten bridge. He could throw all their need for drama right back in their faces.

Until he tripped. His lace had caught on a part of the rope, and Nate was sent flying. He never had learned to tie them properly, something that never mattered until today. The panic set in that moment as he headed towards the snakes. He could see them all, lifting their heads, almost as if they were waiting for him. Their vile skin and rotten tongues just itching for new blood. He thought it was over.

But somehow, he threw out a hand and managed to grab onto the lowest rope, even as his shoe fell to the ground. People watched in open-mouthed fascination as this out-of-shape guy, who had done nothing but laze around the house since the competition started, found the strength to hold on like Sylvester Stallone in *Cliffhanger*.

While some were fascinated by Nate's heavy breathing as he was holding on for dear life, others were more interested in the commentaries. On the more serious one, the psychiatrist Denis Kavolkan was analysing where most people got their fear of snakes from and how it was different to other phobias about creatures that could kill us. Things were a lot lighter with the comedic duo of "Sam and Stan's Wheel of Random". They were continually referencing *Snakes on a Plane* and Indiana Jones, wondering whether being called a snake or a rat was worse and guessing how many people knew what the snake was called in *The Jungle Book*. Right now, though, both shows were asking the same question. Just how long could Nate hold on?

Nate was wondering this himself. He had heard stories about women who had found something in them to lift a car off a child or regular people who had found some adrenalin to beat up someone twice their size. But holding on was one thing. He knew he would have to find even more strength to get himself back onto the rope. He wasn't sure he had that strength. He was barely holding on as it was.

But maybe that was it. He knew how TV worked. The hero, golden shot moment. Any moment now, someone would come along and save him from the hell of falling into a pit of snakes. He just had to hold on. If only his fingers weren't so exhausted. They felt raw, what with all the clinging on they had done so far.

He screamed for life, for mercy. "I can't hold on for long, you need to help, anyone. I can't…I can't…" He knew there was a good chance there was a good Samaritan in there. There had to be, statistically as much as anything.

He had laughed at those kind souls who did things for no motive. Life was too short for that. Now, he would happily give all his money away to whoever could save him. If he wasn't struggling to hold on, he would have been on his hands and knees. Maybe this was another turning point to help him become a better person. Surely, there must be at least one hero from those watching!

There might well have been, had there been someone there. Had Nate got a closer look, he would have seen that those "people" had not moved an inch since they had been placed there as cardboard cut-outs before he had arrived. Selina had chuckled as she wondered how long it would take him to realise. She and the team had thought about something higher-tech, but there was a charm to its simplicity, as borne out by the high number of viewers who had applied for their face to be on the cut-out, along with a signature gesture and vocal catchphrase or sound effect that would go off at random moments.

And so, Nate hung on for dear life, wondering why there was no movement. Nothing was happening. No rescue team. All he could hear were different forms of laughter and various sounds of suspense, interspersed with sounds of the snakes.

Suddenly, he felt the weight collapse, and the lower rope swung back towards the roof he had started on. People watched on in pure fascination as this sluggish New Yorker with no discernible athletic skills flew across the sky, closer than ever to falling in.

But Nate really was hanging on, despite his exhausted body screaming for respite. He found strength and resolve he never knew he had. All he needed now was someone to come along. Nate screamed out for help, but there was still no response. His eyes darted around, seeing everything and yet nothing. He had no idea how much time passed while he held on for dear life, but he reasoned it had to be at least an hour. Maybe more.

Suddenly, the loudspeaker had come on again, reading more details about Felicity's fall from grace. She really had gone into a dark place after they had broken up. Really dark. His concentration began to wander, and his fingers were starting to lose grip. He had nothing left. With a slow dawning realisation, he knew there would be no salvation.

His fingers finally gave out, and he fell backwards into the snakes, screaming so loud viewers reached to lower the volume. Nate reasoned that if he didn't have to look at the snakes, it wouldn't be so bad. Not for the first time that day, he was wrong.

But it wasn't just him. 32% of people had thought he would cross the bridge and in a bonus poll, 77% had gambled he would last longer on the final rope than 4 minutes and 22 seconds. Those disappointed took consolation that they weren't in that pit. You didn't need to have a phobia to find the idea rather unappealing.

BREAK

Selina watched all of it with interest. She looked at her watch and smiled as things had mostly gone to plan. She hadn't legislated for Nate to hang on after falling off the bridge, but that was one of the pleasant surprises that made this job so worthwhile. It was a visual age, and the image of a hapless contestant swinging above a pit of snakes was glorious. As was that moment when he finally let go, that split second just before he fell in, and then his terrified face as he was forced to open his eyes.

If only he had been able to apologise. He'd certainly had enough time. It was the least Felicity deserved.

With only one challenge left, Selina was in an unusually reflective mood. Her devoted team was analysing ratings, the betting patterns, message boards and the feeds of prominent TV critics. So far, the feedback had been less controversial than on the previous challenge. While plenty had loved the idea and the speech just before Denzel was rescued, there had been criticism that the former athlete had spent too long inside and further complaints that visually it lacked flair. That's why she had been happy to see Nate's name come up. She knew this one ticked all the boxes. A fighting chance for the contestant, a chance for redemption, a sense of danger and big points for style and originality.

Though now out of date, she picked up different newspapers and print-outs of online reviewers who had been frenzied in their comments since the gameshow's inception. While most had focused on the six contestants, the challenges themselves (including a whole raft of inaccurate guesses for upcoming punishments) and what it said about society, she noted with a wry smile the focus on her. She had thought that doing an interview in which she refused to give much detail about her personal life would quieten down the angle of her being mysterious and elusive, but instead, it only seemed to pique people's curiosity.

She had no idea why. Reading the features, they seemed to range from her "terrifying staff as she banged on an ivory desk" to "cold and detached who only showed affection to her dogs Donner and Blitzen". It couldn't be more wrong. Her three children were perfectly happy, as were her husband and her two dogs, though they were Dachshunds, not Labradors as quoted.

Perhaps that was the consequence of not letting her staff talk to the press unofficially. She set high standards and certainly didn't suffer fools. But she was neither a volatile firecracker nor a remote ice queen. She'd met male and female colleagues who resembled each stereotype but hated that people tended to be pigeonholed in such tight parameters. Some people preferred their celebrities as one-dimensional beings.

She picked up her first trophy and remembered her acceptance speech. The doubters had been patronising and dismissive, believing she would fall flat on her face before she had even finished renovating her new head office. Even worse, they had assumed she hadn't even earned the position but had slept her way to the top. She'd rammed their baseless resentment back down their throats, even given a thinly veiled reference before she left the stage. Since then, two with shameless nerves had asked for a job, one tried to hire her (for a lower salary, no less), while another had suggested a merger. Pride and stupidity certainly made for a fun mix, something she noted with a wry chuckle when she'd sent them all packing.

It had all started with *Dancing with Dreams*. It wasn't reinventing the wheel, just a simple show about regular people being taught to dance to their favourite song by a caring professional dancer. Judging by the sunken body language and desperate pleading of its creator, IPPR had clearly been last on the list.

"I'm telling you, there's something there!" its pitcher Gordon Woods had emphasised, as he handed over three different sets of documents, each varying in size. "You'll find three different summaries. I wasn't sure how much time you could see me for, so I came prepared."

Selina had looked at the lanky and pale-skinned gentleman in front of her. She looked closely at his body language, that internal struggle of trying to radiate confidence even when he had little left after countless setbacks. According to her sources from other companies, he hadn't even been able to get through the door of some, while others had thrown him out to uproarious laughter for such a dull concept.

And yet, despite his noticeable insecurity, he was still here. Selina admired that and told herself she would listen to his pitch with utmost manners, no matter the quality of his presentation.

"The three documents cover the different possible budgets," explained Gordon, almost knocking over the table in his awkwardness but composing himself for a more impassioned tone. "I know it's a dancing show without any celebrities, but I don't want a programme that competes with the glitz and glamour, but rather one that has its own path. Why not a show about real people getting the chance to meet a talented professional dancer? At first, you'll get the two left feet visual gags and the professional dancer needing the patience of a saint, but then you'll see the bonding between the two and then that special moment when they dance for their actual partner, whether that's a spouse, family member or whatever."

Selina had actually been intrigued since the beginning, but had wanted to see how good his pitch was and just how well he would deal with the pressure. Gordon hadn't said anything about his living situation, but she could sense that if she said no, he was done with the industry. Probably to move out of his parent's basement or some rat-infested tiny apartment and back to the stability of a job he had the qualifications and parental approval for, if no genuine interest in. Selina was enthusiastic in her interest, and all the contract stuff was finalised within a few days.

It had been a smash success and broken network ratings for the previously unfashionable Tuesday 8 pm slot. There were many noteworthy moments. A bullied teen finding a more confident version of himself to successfully ask out his next-door neighbour, having spent months rehearsing flamboyant moves to her favourite musician. A closeted adult mustering up the courage to come out, her bravery also reflected by her pride in losing her inhibitions on the dancefloor and learning to love her body for the first time. Estranged cousins reunited again after one of them had heard a song on the radio they'd both loved growing up and determined to bring those memories back.

But there was no denying the crowning moment. When a war veteran had a terminal diagnosis, he felt it was time to thank his wife for the years she had spent nursing him. His wife had not been a professional carer but had done everything possible to learn about his disease and the scientific, emotional and practical elements needed to understand it. His memory was failing, his body was falling to pieces, but his passion to learn the song he had danced with his wife on their wedding day 52 years ago was undimmed.

"Thank you for everything," they had both said to their dancer, who couldn't stop himself from crying. Usually a perfectionist, he had been worried he would come across as too critical in the final performance. But even though the pace was slow, the rhythm not quite to the music and the footwork clumsy, he couldn't have been prouder of his 78-year-old prodigy.

The fact that the husband passed even before the show aired made the Emmy a certainty. Selina wasn't the type to gloat, but if she was, she would have waited until after *Sinners, Saints and Seadogs* had finished top of its timeslot in only its third episode. The sitcom about reckless pirates seemed to be loathed by everyone important, but the ratings were impressive, and everyone seemed to love its two main stars, even before they started dating in real life. There had been something about it that had just jumped out when she saw the premise. No one ever thought of a pirate ship as a great place for a sitcom, but she knew with the right actors and production team, it would be a hit. The show's creators still sent her a Christmas card every year and flowers on her birthday.

Needing a break from the incessant focus on *Wheel of Phobia*, she looked at other recent shows that had brought her glory.

Disaster Dogs and Chaotic Cats was about how much mess a group of excitable young pets could make in an hour. It was made for a relative pittance but had struck gold with its audience, helped by an attractive and energetic presenter, competitive pet owners and a madcap scoring system. "The bigger the mess, the bigger the prize," was soon a household expression, and the pet clothing line was quite the earner. That was the show that got the most fan mail, too.

Paige Turners was all about two different novelists each week who champion a beloved book from their childhood to an age-appropriate group of children. Whoever got the most votes from the children in the studio got a book-shaped trophy, while the loser had to press the lever to slime the amiable and stylish (and admittedly gorgeous) hostess Paige Masterson. While the literary angle was appreciated and commended, there was no denying the weekly sliming really got the bigger views online. Selina's rivals at the network had laughed when she had commissioned the show, but they weren't laughing now. The fact three different networks had cancelled the shows they had put in the same timeslot wasn't lost on her, either.

The acclaimed adaptions of Arthur Ashe, Thomas Edison, Jim Thorpe, Guy Fawkes and Hitler's final days all added to her aura, as had keeping two shows on the air when it looked like they had run out of steam. In the soap's case, she had made vast changes, in the other she hadn't changed anything other than its timeslot and some improved promotion.

Underperforming stars were out, no matter their fame or reputation. "Gardener to the stars" Phil Gardiner was out two weeks before celebrating 30 years on the network. His ratings hadn't even dropped too badly, but she hadn't liked the way he treated the interns or refused to give credit to anyone from the team in interviews. He was gone; news of his firing timed to help distract people from the cancellation of an underperforming reality show with a small but vocal audience.

People would act as though she had made a Faustian pact, cast a witches' spell or had a fairy godmother and genie locked in her cupboard. The truth was all rather prosaic. Beneath the fancy graphics and dazzling presentations, it came down to this. Had something similar been done? If so, which parts had been successful and which had failed? Who would it be appealing to? How much would it cost, and how long to produce? Who could they get to do it? Was there anything about it that would provide any talking points? Not to mention reading everyone's proposals and ensuring they felt comfortable enough to come back with a better idea. Sure, often the follow-up ideas were worse, but that wasn't her fault. And that 95% perspiration was worth it for that 5% inspiration.

She had explained it to her team at different points, and they would act like she was holding something back, like she really knew the secret recipe of Coke or the final burial place of Amelia Earhart. Maybe it was like the Angel of Mons, which took on a life of its own during the First World War, even though its writer kept reminding people the story was fictional. If people were happy with the illusion, she was happy to provide it.

But while she had mastered comedy, period drama, scripted Saturday night entertainment and the arts, she had really lacked a seminal gameshow. What she loved about them was that they were so quick and cheap to make. There was never a shortage of idiots. As well as guaranteeing the giveaways were minimal, it gave countless opportunities for people to laugh at those severely lacking in popular culture or basic knowledge. The world was a small place when things went viral.

But this gameshow was so different. So many twists, turns and controversies. Rewriting all the rules and leaving its rivals for dust. And there were still so many surprises left.

V

Madison felt uneasy as she surveyed the eerie scene in front of her. What once had seemed crowded, with the sound of Denzel in the gym, Linda playing guitar and Jed muttering while reading, now felt apocalyptic.

Nate had been such a slob, yet now he was gone, the tidiness once so valued seemed worthless. His devotion to his basketball team and his video games may not have connected with her, but it still felt fun to see someone happy over small things. She was going to miss his energy and humour. She wondered how he had gotten on with the challenge, then reasoned it was best not to think about it.

Instead, she started thinking about the fact there were now only two of them left. Madison had never played professional sports or cared for them. But her parents had always been big tennis fans, active members of their local country club, and noticeably disappointed she and her brothers never shared their love for the game. That hadn't stopped them taking her and her brothers to visit Evert's tennis academy in Florida, hoping it would spark something. It hadn't, but she had always been interested in Evert's rivalry with Martina Navratilova, her equal on the court but polar opposite in terms of background and lifestyle. While they had begun the tournament as rivals keeping out of each other's way, by the end there was a mutual respect that led to a solid friendship in retirement. Maybe the gameshow would lead to something similar with Yasmeen. After all, they were the only ones left stuck in this Frankenstein-style circus.

She got an immediate answer when Yasmeen followed her into the bedroom with a determined expression. Without saying anything, Yasmeen immediately picked up her two suitcases and carried them out of the room. Returning from the men's bedroom, the influencer carried her only remaining possessions, her Pilates mat and some candles. Pausing at the door she said simply, "It's easier this way, you know, right?" and left before Madison could say anything.

Yasmeen hadn't noticed Madison's shocked expression, but she wouldn't have reacted any different to the heiress even if she had. With Nate gone, the place would be quieter and tidier. And she could finally have her own room. Fully aware of Nate's slovenly reputation, she had largely stayed away from the men's bedroom. She just couldn't understand how someone could live like that. With the basketball posters all gone, the wardrobe empty and the floor spotless, it was as though no one had ever been in there. Which made it perfect.

Yasmeen put her things down carefully and lay down, staring up at the ceiling as it began to hit her. There had been five people standing in her way. Now there was just one. In the real world, she would back herself to intimidate or outsmart Daddy's little rich girl. She'd done it several times to opponents over the years. She didn't have a fancy education, but she definitely knew street smarts. Even as a youngster, she'd known how to spot the weakness of someone standing in her way. Sometimes, that was by a sly comment here and there, other times something more devious.

But here, it was different. Not just because there were camera operators everywhere. Unlike the others who seemed to get used to them, Yasmeen could never fully relax. One time, she signed the cameras with a Spanish swear word, while another time she had pushed the cameraman when he saw her waiting too closely outside the bathroom she was coming out of. She was never afraid of anyone or the consequences of standing up to people.

She didn't mind being the bad girl, the rebel, the wildcard. When people saw her piercings and tattoos and dyed hair, that's what they always assumed anyway. The truth was that she didn't see it as a form of protest against society or as a way of being left alone by narrow-minded people. Every tattoo meant something. She had seven, mostly on her right arm. Three were lyrics from songs, each representing love, joy or hope. One was a butterfly she'd seen on a day she cut school. The fifth one was her first motorbike, before she'd crashed it and couldn't afford to get it fixed. The sixth was the logo of her first Pilates studio. The seventh, which had actually been the first one she'd had done, was one she never discussed.

Her love of hair changes and piercings was all about her love for when she looked in the mirror. Despite the constant emphasis on her looks, weight and overall body shape, she liked how she looked. She knew how severe the consequences were for those who didn't. When she turned up for an audition to be in an aspiring rock band's new video, she'd heard the outrageously vicious comments said out loud to the girls. And the damage they were bound to cause. She took great satisfaction in throwing water all over their amps and smashing the lead singer's guitar. She took even greater pleasure when years later, she discovered they were in soulless jobs, having failed miserably in their rock and roll dream.

Though she'd been accused of being ruthless with competitors, she'd always encouraged body positivity and blocked followers who said anything personal about others, not just her. Even then, it was just drops in the ocean. Sure, she'd enjoyed sabotaging the careers of rival pods, but that was just business. Most of them deserved it.

She missed the outdoors. All the air conditioning in the world couldn't equate to the feeling of fresh air on a sunny day when she could go for a long walk. She never understood how people could just sit in an office all day, especially if they weren't near a window. She'd once had a summer job as a temp and quit after two hours. Instead, she'd worked in a field picking fruit. Sure, it wasn't glamourous, but it was in nature, with people who wouldn't smirk when she entered a room or look down on her.

She had nothing really against Madison, even if her name was ridiculously fancy. Sure, she was a super-rich kid, but it wasn't like she'd turned up with an expensive handbag or outrageously expensive jewellery. In fact, apart from her classy clothes and shoes, the only thing she wore that hinted at her wealth was a necklace with the initials ML. An 18th birthday present was the obvious guess. Yasmeen wasn't sure what her favourite birthday present was. There had been few memorable ones. That's why, even when she'd had more money than she knew what to do with, she rarely did anything special. She'd get embarrassed whenever any former boyfriends or girlfriends did anything extravagant for her. She took out her book on Spanish poetry and worked on her pronunciation.

Madison was writing in her diary. Though most people used it at the end of their day, here the 35-year-old just wrote whenever she felt like it. Sometimes that was once a day, sometimes as much as three or four. Apart from precious few minutes in the bathroom, it was the only privacy she had in the whole process. Every other moment, she knew she was being judged by people desperate for controversy or else just an escape from their own lives. She knew from experience one way to make yourself feel better was to compare yourself with someone else worse off.

Like Yasmeen, she wasn't interested in small talk but would have liked the option. But all things considered, it was probably for the best. Madison had kept all signs of wealth to a discrete minimum, but she could still see that resentment whenever Madison spent too long looking at her clothes. It wasn't a look she saw often in the circles she moved in, but there was no disguising it. That was probably part of her opponent's persona. A warning not to push it. Almost like a dog snarling not to get too close to the fence, or there would be major consequences.

While all this was going on, Selina had a rueful smile. Watching the two so guarded was like two boxers circling each other just before the first bell rang. The question as to when to sound that bell was one that she'd been debating with her team. With only two challenges needing to be ready at the same time, it was relatively straightforward, and things could be ready at short notice. But though things were quiet, she was enjoying it.

As were viewers at home. Viewers were firmly in one camp or the other. Those in #TeamMadison loved her class, style and intelligence. They admired her for the way she was trying to reinvent herself when she had enough money to go to some far-off tropical island and never be bothered again. They felt protective of her when she lowered her guard romantically, only to almost fall for a playboy with an awful history. And they found her mild goofiness appealing.

#TeamYasmeen or the #YasmeenDreamers, as they called themselves, were all about breaking through glass ceilings and brick walls. Yasmeen was a Street Fighter. She'd grown up in poverty that plenty of her followers recognised. But rather than settle for a job she never wanted, she had scrapped, fairly and unfairly, to the top. She never would have found herself suckered in like Madison had. They were all about self-expression and not caring what those with narrow minds and limited ambition thought.

The fact that the two women had little to say to one another almost ramped up the appeal. Selina wasn't a huge boxing fan, but she knew the best fights came from hatred. She hated all that hugging and mutual respect at the end. She wanted her fighters to give everything because the idea of losing was so repugnant. She wanted something more than sport. She wanted war.

Two days passed, largely without incident. Selina had mischievously sounded a different kind of alarm, which had the two panicking. Within a few seconds, she had clarified it was a false alarm relating to "security issues", but she had enjoyed the reaction. Both had sworn, Madison in despair and Yasmeen in defiance.

But it became obvious something had to give. While most people preferred the moment on a rollercoaster when it went down, Selina loved the anticipation, not knowing when it was going to change. That's why she always kept her eyes closed when on one, which, to her frustration, her husband would always assume was due to fear.

Waiting until Madison was in the shower and Yasmeen was having cereal, she pressed the klaxon. Aware of how nervous she had come across before, Madison was determined not to look flustered again. She carried on her shower as though she hadn't heard anything and finished at her own pace. In truth, her stuff had been packed and ready to go since she walked through the door after Nate's exit. She decided to finish the chapter she was reading on Slyvia Plath before waiting by the door. She'd been ready for days now.

Yasmeen stared into the distance as she decided to leave her cereal, before throwing the spoon into the sink near where she had stood next to the table. She went for a final walk around the flat, wishing she could take some photos. She would never take her ability to leave her house for granted again. They could tell themselves they had done a great job because they'd given her vegan food and clean conditions, but it had been like living in a zoo. Worse, really, because of her annoying companions.

Noticing that Madison was there, she waited until Selina had arrived before making her way to the door. She wryly noted Selina was wearing black and thought about saying something, but seeing Selina's subtle smirk, decided to stay calm.

Selina walked them to the studio, though the cameramen walked behind her, all military precision amidst the pomp and ceremony. Even the entrance music had changed, all majestic and retro at the same time. The noise seemed louder, too. That wasn't a coincidence. Selina had increased the audience size within the studio through several means, including smaller chairs, less studio space and a looser interpretation of the fire safety code.

Buck may have had less space to work in, but he just loved an audience. The bigger, the better. Though he'd initially valued the space to walk around in, several episodes in he'd wished there were more people. He did his best work when he had a bigger energy to work with. Rock stars got big arenas; why couldn't he? It wasn't like he was going to play all the classics plus some forgettable new stuff. In his shows, no joke, or even a suit, was used twice.

"People, it's been a hell of a ride," he bellowed to his ecstatic audience. "And we're almost at the end. Have you enjoyed it so far? Is this, or is this not, the greatest gameshow ever?"

The audience bellowed in unison, like the world was about to end. It was so loud that both contestants covered their ears, but Buck wanted it even louder.

"I didn't hear you the first time!" he screamed, ramping up the energy as though it was needed to power the whole arena. And the crowd responded to their leader by making the 4,000 sound like 40,000.

"I told you when it started it was going to be special. I promised, didn't I? And I kept it. It's been one heck of a journey."

And in his shimmering golden suit with dollar signs featuring prominently as part of the design, he strutted down to meet Madison and Yasmeen.

"There was once six walking through those doors," roared Buck. "Now there's only two. Very soon, there will be one. Let's meet them for the final time," grinned the excitable host, as he basked in the applause. He generously gestured towards the two, letting them share in the audience's devotion.

It wasn't because he respected them. Far from it. He wasn't the slightest bit bothered about their fate and had nothing but contempt for celebrities who took their fame for granted. Having read all the regularly updated notes prepared by the producers, the contestants all seemed a stupid and worthless bunch. Buck knew he had that skill of being able to insult people either without them knowing about it or being able to challenge it. People thought it was God-given. Like hell it was! He'd had to work at it. He studied all the body language of actors and comedians who had charisma. He'd read all the books about aspiring entertainers, how they'd stayed motivated through the crappy jobs they'd had to do before they made it big and how they were able to take advantage on the lookout for showbiz opportunities. He had utter contempt for the six for throwing that all away.

That's why he ensured he was nice to people he met, especially when he was on camera. It wasn't too difficult, really. Even if it was tiring at times when out getting groceries, he did enjoy the adoration. He had never forgotten the days when he was honing his craft. The times he was ignored. One day, he had gone on after a ventriloquist and actually got fewer laughs.

He had no great love for his work crew. They had such simple lives, and they clung to his exciting life with such embarrassing desperation. Buck was astute enough though to throw some crumbs their way every once in a while. It's good to let them play with the king for a few hours, he reasoned. That's why every year, he'd have a party at his beach house with invites to all his team, including ones he struggled to remember the names of.

Madison looked classy in a grey dress that looked straightforward but was one of the more expensive ones she owned. If this tacky experiment was going to end in disaster, at least she would go out looking sophisticated, like a modern-day Grace Kelly. Yasmeen was wearing a Ramones t-shirt. She took great joy in correcting people who just assumed she pretended to like them because they were cool. She'd been listening to them for years. While waiting for the security guards to arrive, she'd been listening to the Rocket to Russia album. Unlike previous shows, she knew she might need that defiant anger.

"So, Madison, give us a few words about your experiences on the show," Buck asked with extravagant enthusiasm. "Has it been like you expected?"

"It's been…" Madison paused as she wondered what word to use. She'd used so many different ones in her diary, choosing one should have been easy. "Well, for one, I'm still here, so that's good. I've been able to connect more with myself, hopefully connect with the audience and realise I am tough enough to be on this show. I know my family wasn't the only one unsure if I could survive."

"Well, it's not over yet," chuckled Buck, but softened it with a smile and a hug. "You have to be proud of what you've achieved so far. What's been the toughest part for you so far?"

"I have missed a lot of things. Family, friends, the routine of regular life. I definitely miss my watch! But hey, it's good to get out of your comfort zone. It's given me the chance to get to know five people I wouldn't otherwise have met. And that's been fun," said Madison, trying to remain positive.

"And that's a great attitude to have," nodded Buck, though he recognised the insincerity. Her needing to play the fake gratitude game was probably the only thing he'd admired about her. He hated everything that spoilt rich trust-fund kid represented. But today wasn't going to let anything bother him. He wasn't surprised the show had been a huge revelation. Sure, not everyone had loved it, but a little controversy was good. All of his favourite comedians walked on the wild side a little. His agent had been buzzing with new opportunities. Before, companies had wanted him for silly suncream ads, or random things like roast potatoes, detergent or kitchen paper. Now they were talking casinos, gin and maybe even aftershave. He really was big-time.

"Now, let's get onto our Blitzkrieg Pop, or should that be Punk girl," said Buck with a slick smile, as he motioned towards Yasmeen. "I haven't listened to them in a while, but good to see The Ramones' spirit alive and well. The whole gameshow is almost over. You're either going to walk away a winner, with added fame, money and prestige. Or you're going to have lost out on everything, having come so close and nothing to show for it. Describe how you're feeling to everyone here."

"Well, if I win, then life is going to change big time. There are so many big plans. I want to launch my own spiritual retreat. A place for people to relax and learn more about the natural world around us. Life is stressful. I want people to learn about the beauties of Pilates in a safe and loving place. Next to it, I'd have an animal shelter. A huge open space for the animals to roam. Different ones in different parts of the country. People could adopt the ones they like. And I'd also like to promote veganism. There are so many misconceptions about how you can only get protein from meat. If I could franchise a sports team, I could reach out to players and fans."

"Those are big plans," said Buck, very surprised. "I've gotta say, if I won that money, the first thing I'd do is hide it from my wife," he said, to laughter from everyone. "I'm kidding people, I'm kidding." But he couldn't stop the laughter. "My wife would totally want half, and there'd be tons of stuff to buy for the kids. So, with my 3% of the win, I'd totally get a big TV for every room and then hire someone as a human remote. One hand for him to change the channels, with a freshly cold beer in the other. That would be sweeeeet!"

Selina looked on with a smile. Buck just knew how to set the tone of the show. Yasmeen's sickly-sweet answer had threatened to take the vibe in the wrong place, but Buck knew how to shut it down. The show's popularity didn't come from generating sympathy; it was about creating drama. The executive had ensured Buck had never seen any of the challenges or had any idea what they were about. She knew he'd never get attached to the contestants, but his joyful ignorance meant he was always looking forwards, not backwards. And the big moment was coming.

"And how will you feel if you don't win?"

Yasmeen swore a few times, but playfully and with more of a smile than she might have done earlier in the competition. For one, she hadn't lost yet, and she didn't want to look stupid if she did end up winning. For another, she really hadn't processed the thought of what might happen.

She'd worked hard on her positive outlook, but really her main feeling, rather than fear, was impatience.

"Our apologies for anyone offended by the bad language used there," Buck said in forced politeness. He hated having to apologise for something that wasn't his fault and something he didn't see as a problem in the first place. It was actually pretty funny. A world without comedy wasn't a world at all.

Madison looked over in interest, and she knew that Yasmeen was thinking the same thing she was. No more questions, no more delays. They'd come this far. All they wanted now was for that wheel to spin, and it could all be over one way or another.

"Well, I think they've waited long enough," said Buck with a deliberately long pause, as he glanced at them both to heighten the suspense. "Yes, that's right... It's time for the betting patterns!"

Buck had an extra spring in his step as he moved closer to the betting board, though he was sure to have a quick glance at the two contestants. "With only two left, you know these numbers better add up to 100," he joked and fell about laughing. He then stopped and pointed to the screen. "There really isn't much in it, is there?"

Madison Larouche 49.2% and Yasmeen Kahley 50.8%.

There was a real buzz in the audience as they realised how tight it was. Some of the audience even had t-shirts specially made. The fact that the groups weren't segregated only added to the appeal, particularly as it was roughly an even split. Buck had ensured the animosity had been ramped up with a financial incentive for the warm-up act, so much so that three people had been thrown out for violence. Rather than be appalled, Selina had relished it.

Madison never knew what to make of the numbers. She had no real idea if she was liked or hated or even if people felt indifferent towards her. Yasmeen never took any notice. All that mattered was that that wheel kept off her name.

"I can tell you that the overall betting for this final increased 44% on last time. Big, big numbers. Incredible, really! We love how you've embraced this show. We wanted to do something different. And we've done it. This show would be nothing without you. Take a bow, everyone. The guys here and the guys watching, well, wherever you're watching. We're grateful to you all."

Responding to instructions in his ear, he knew it was time to draw lots. Madison and Yasmeen did it in a composed way, Yasmeen quickly, as though the cylinder was about to close. While it was looking as though she was being impatient, Yasmeen knew there was no point hanging around. There had only been one ball left, after all.

Madison Lerouch: White 5
Yasmeen Kahley: Yellow 6

"This is it, people, the final spin! But before we do, one final surprise."

Madison and Yasmeen were both appalled. How many shocks were needed? Even Selina was taken aback. She was in charge, after all. She was supposed to know everything.

Buck pretended to blow a trumpet. "A warm round of applause, everybody. We have a special guest to come on down."

People wondered who it could be. A celebrity? A former contestant? Or even someone random from the crowd, chosen earlier? The crowd was looking at each other. Madison and Yasmeen kept quiet but wondered if it was someone they both knew. Or something to do with the upcoming challenge.

It was none of those. To great anticipation, a scrawny, pale 18-year-old teenager came down the stairs and into the studio, with his hands in his pockets and a slightly shy demeanour. With his beanie cap, poorly maintained skin and slumped posture, he was like your stereotypical teenager. Certainly not a lover of the spotlight. Yet here he was, walking towards the stage. Everyone was curious about what was happening until Buck gave him a big hug.

"Everyone, I have the honour of introducing you to my son, Jason. It's his birthday today, so I thought I'd give him a front-row seat to the best show in town. And the honour of launching the final spin."

Selina should have been annoyed. She discouraged spontaneity and rebellion. But the crowd loved the gesture, and in the grand scheme of things, it had worked out well. Much as she liked to pretend otherwise, it was impossible to fully control Buck. She knew no one else could do the job as well as him, and if you reined him in too tight, you'd lose that flamboyant spark and instinctive energy.

Buck was a father, but he was also a showman and didn't let his monosyllabic teen steal the show. Jason smiled a bit, said how lucky he was to be Buck's son, wished both contestants luck and then spun the wheel. During the excitement of the wheel being spun, he was quietly nudged offstage. You may get to share the limelight with Buck for a moment, but that was all.

The spin went on. People watching wondered if it was for longer, but further checks carried out later proved it was the same time. Selina had thought about lengthening it but rightly assumed people were suspicious enough anyway that it would only fuel conspiracy rumours.

During the spin, the cameras showed a little of Buck doing some smooth dancing gestures and the crowd going wild. Mostly though, it followed Madison's increasingly futile attempts to stay calm and Yasmeen mouthing the lyrics to *I Wanna Be Sedated*.

With the fact that every place on the wheel was either the white of Madison or the yellow of Yasmeen, it certainly was an action-packed minute. But it had to end, and it certainly had to end badly for one of the contestants.

Just as Yasmeen was reaching the lyrics about not being able to control her fingers or toes, it landed on yellow. People wondered how the rebellious star would react, but those who knew her well or who had followed her since the show started wouldn't have been surprised by a simple, loud cursing. There really wasn't more to say.

When Buck asked her how she was feeling, Yasmeen sighed. "Life sucks sometimes. So it goes. The money would have been nice, but yeah, it is what it is."

When Buck asked her if she was ready for her upcoming challenge, she just shrugged. She waved to her crowd and shook hands with an embarrassed Madison, who avoided her gaze. Yasmeen calmly walked to the edge of the studio without looking back. It was never good to look back. It was one of her mantras, which once led to Nate joking that's why she was so bad at parallel parking.

"Hey everyone, I'm Yasmeen Kahley," said a voice trying to be soft, but it was clearly a tone she rarely used. "I'm here because I've screwed up, basically. Not just once, yeah, but several times. I know that some of you can't see past my mistakes. Yes, it was me who ruined the ending to the final instalment of the Galactic Treasure franchise. As I said countless times, I thought I was sending a message to my closest friend. I had no idea I was sending it to everyone.

"The time I trashed that guy's car, I really thought he was pretending to be disabled. I had no idea that his condition meant that he could actually walk short distances. I was ignorant; I had to go and learn some more. Once I read all about it, I apologised for damaging his car and the things I called him. I know he took it personal, but it wasn't meant to be. When I get mad, I shoot my mouth off. I've worked hard to keep it under control, but I don't always get it right.

"I know I hurt a lot of people with my book. I really did set out as a form of cleansing, a closure to my previous life. But I was angry, and that anger came across in the book. The way I described former lovers was bad, and I know I hurt and embarrassed them. I've worked on my anger a lot. I've been to therapy; I've tried out different meditations until I found the one that worked best for me. I know my parents tried their best. I could have been more sensitive. Wow, that's the most I've ever said, ever. I feel like one of those dolls my grandmother used to play with that had a string at the back." And then a long pause as she looked directly to the camera. "I just want to be forgiven."

Yasmeen was out of the studio by the time it was being played, but she wouldn't have learned anything from watching it back. She remembered what she'd said, especially the last sentence. For once, she'd really let her guard down. The money would be great, but she already knew what it was like to be poor. Unlike Linda, she hated making poverty part of her identity. It always annoyed her how much interviewers liked to focus on it.

She'd lost a lot of money when she was sued, but really, it was the anger people had towards her that affected her most. She couldn't get a coffee without people staring at her, shouting things, filming her every move. And when she replied back with that same tone, people said she was the crazy, bitter one. Her subscribers fell, and her comments section got even nastier.

The 29-year-old would have been interested in the reaction to her speech. What was clear was just how much loathing there was for her for blowing the ending to that movie, even four years on. Her other mistakes might have been forgiven. She knew how messed up family life was for a lot of people. She wasn't the first person to slag off her parents. The fact she'd admitted to going to therapy was worth a lot of points. The things about the former boyfriends, and one ex-girlfriend, weren't good. But as she made clear, she wasn't in a great place herself at the time, and the stuff she said about herself was far worse. She wasn't trying to be nasty about them and had thought she'd been vague enough no one would be able to work things out. But people had, and those were the excerpts that made the headlines.

The thing was, despite what everyone said, she wasn't trying to get even with them. There was just so much rage. They'd just got caught up in the crossfire.

But that movie would follow her around forever. It was the sixth one of an epic saga, and it had been talked about for months. She'd only got a ticket to the premiere because she was in a casual relationship with someone close to one of the producers. And what was forgotten about in everything was that people had later forwarded it on. If they had kept it to themselves, the wider public wouldn't have known.

All these thoughts and more were going through her head as she was being driven to her fate. It had been the same car as the other four challenges, and the same security. The competition had so many variables, Selina liked to keep things simple whenever possible.

The Pilates Punk Princess, as she had once been called, knew the cameras would want tears or anger. But the truth was, maybe this was how it had to end. Close enough to success to actually touch it, but far enough away that she never had it even to begin with.

As a child she never hoped, she just focused on actions. Why save up for a bicycle she could never afford when it was easier to steal one? Why study for a job she would never be fully qualified for? Better to sabotage the chances of everyone else in that waiting room. They would always have other chances. She had to make her own luck.

She was disrupted from her thoughts by a phone call. She already knew it was going to be Selina. It couldn't have been anyone else.

"As you are aware, you are now out of the gameshow, and you will be facing your challenge soon," said a voice devoid of any warmth, something that Yasmeen was okay with. She hated fake politeness. She knew she was in trouble, and hearing a friendly voice would only have added to the farce.

"Do I at least get a clue?" Yasmeen asked in hope more than expectation.

"Your challenge is still being prepared," Selina said, ignoring what she saw as Yasmeen's pointless question. "Once the challenge is completed, you can leave. Do not consider trying to communicate with anyone else in the building. They have temporarily been relocated." With that, the phone went dead and was handed back to one of the massive security guards. She didn't know why there were so many. It's not like she was ever violent. Something Selina would have known when she was researching her life.

Yasmeen didn't say anything else during the car ride. It could have ridden until doomsday; she wasn't going to say anything. In fact, she was so exhausted that she fell asleep there and then. She hated falling asleep in public as much as using restaurant bathrooms. But these were no ordinary circumstances. She had no strength left.

Yasmeen had no idea how long she was out for. All she knew was that when she woke up, she felt joy. Not because of a change of attitude. She knew she was in big trouble. She prided herself on never letting herself become deluded, no matter how desperate the situation. This was the last challenge, so it was going to have to be something spectacular.

But she couldn't help but smile as she saw her apartment building. It wasn't as big as the one she had just been in, but she didn't care. She loved her New York building. What did she care about batting cages, video games and personal gyms? She had missed her apartment so much. It wasn't huge, but everything inside meant so much to her.

There was no one in the street, but then, judging by the lack of any real sunlight, it was in the early hours. After being inside for so long, she was happy to have a vague idea of time just judging by the sky. She smiled at the memories of her getting in after a late night of partying and getting judged by those in suits on their way to work. She never understood the contempt. She was making the most out of her life, just as they were. They just did it at different times of the day.

The security guards escorted her to her door, and she was excited and nervous as she reached into her handbag she'd been handed just before entering the car. It seemed only a lifetime ago that she was here in her apartment and yet, it must only have been about a week. Or was it longer? She may as well have been in prison. Even the most mundane of things seemed to make her happy. Seeing a random cat in the street. Noticing that the billboard posters had been updated. That a nearby house had finally finished being repainted.

She wasn't sure what was she expecting when she turned the key and went inside. Friends? Family? Enemies? Instead, it was eerily quiet. Everything was just as she had left it. Spotless. For the first time in a long time, she felt relaxed. She wandered into her different rooms and for the first time forgot about the cameras following her. She was home. She was happy.

Yasmeen was about to put some music on when she saw the note on the fridge.

"Dear Yasmeen. Your challenge will begin tomorrow. Any attempt to leave the flat before then will not be permitted and will result in further punishment."

She should have been annoyed. The TV had had its cables removed. She still didn't have her phone. She couldn't contact anyone. She still didn't know what was going on in the world outside. And she sure didn't like the ominous tone of that note. But Yasmeen had spent so much time worrying that she was going to ensure she enjoyed tonight.

She looked in her fridge and was delighted to see all her favourites were there. Sure, that meant people had been in her flat and she hated that, but hey, she was hungry. At least for one more night, life was good. She'd worry about the other stuff when she woke up tomorrow. And with a great smile, she noticed the large clock above her bed. It was the widest smile she'd had since she'd entered this stupid competition. It was 3.11 am. If it hadn't been so high up on the wall, she would have hugged it. She contented herself with the thought that when she woke up, she would know exactly what time it was.

That was something Selina had been counting on. She waited for 6.02 am exactly before she set off the fire alarm. By that point, the smoke had been building, and the sounds of the flames were building nicely. Selina had hired guys to increase the sound. She wanted Yasmeen frantic. It was all about the drama, the tension, the entertainment. Selina couldn't wait.

Yasmeen awoke to a strange mix of smoke, heat and the sound of flames. She knew even before opening her eyes, this was the challenge. She'd always hated fire, and she knew just where her phobia had come from. As a child, she had been trapped in a high-rise building and at one point didn't think she would get out in time. It was the only time in her life she had been genuinely petrified.

The sound of the flames brought it all back. Yasmeen had to get out. It was terror. Pure terror. She jumped out of her bed and could feel the heat of how bad the fire was. It was so loud and hot and fast. She could sense the flames getting bigger by the minute. She could sense it as much as feel it. The room's temperature was rising. She had to get out!

She ran to the door, but it was locked. Not just closed like it was sometimes, which needed a bit of extra force. This was properly jammed shut. Was this down to the heat increasing the size of the wood?

She started screaming and trying to use that energy to get the door open. It felt like it was bolted down, and the effort forced her back onto the floor. That's when she noticed the actual padlock on the door and a video screen suddenly appearing on the wall.

"The challenge has started. The correct answer must be given before the next question is revealed. Answer every question correctly, and the padlock will be removed."

"And if I don't? I mean if I can't? What then?" She screamed it all out as loud as she could. She knew she was in trouble. She'd never been more scared in her life.

Not just by the flames, but by the fact that she was going to lose this challenge, and she may not get out. Yasmeen was awful at answering questions on gameshows and quiz nights. If you didn't get the right answer, you were stupid or ignorant. How could you not know the capital of Morocco? Or when the Battle of Gettysburg was? She could see the look of disappointment and judgement in people's eyes.

But she wasn't stupid. She'd flopped at school, but so what? It wasn't her knowledge of random rivers or previous presidents that had gotten her famous. It was graft. And skill. And ruthlessness. But right now, her life depended on general knowledge. In this sick and twisted game, she had to concentrate.

The first question then came up in large lettering.

"Question 1. Where were you on Sunday, 14 April 2015?"

That was it. Yasmeen read it four or five times, trying to make sense of it. What was so special about that date? It wasn't her birthday or someone else from her family. It wasn't a national holiday. She knew there were no state holidays in April. There was no big festival or concert she'd been to.

She'd ruled out anything famous, so it had to be something smaller. Something to do with her own life. Shutting her eyes to concentrate, she tried to think what was so special on that day. She would have been 16. She didn't do much on Saturdays. Her mother had tried to get her to take piano lessons that an elderly neighbour offered for free, but she had quit after the third class. She had stolen a skateboard at 14. That had been fun. She'd really seen herself as an Avril Lavigne Sk8er girl and used to do tricks at the local skatepark.

She waved around her hands in frustration as she tried not to panic. The flames were getting hotter, and she knew there was only one way out of her flat. She couldn't fail on the first question. The point was to think of the major things in her life. Ok. First cigarette. That was 13. She hadn't had a joint until 16. Her first drink, a cheap spirit she'd sneaked out of her father's cabinet, was 15. Her first real kiss? That was earlier. She looked at the date again. Could it be connected to that dance competition she went to? But that couldn't be right. That had to have been on a Saturday, not the Sunday. But it was the only thing that seemed remotely connected.

"The Katrina Vanerring Dance Studio." She shouted it out, thinking if she sounded confident enough, that alone would convince them.

The screen immediately went dark. Did she only get one guess? That didn't seem fair. That wasn't written in the instructions. She was about to swear when the screen came back on.

"Question 2. What sandwiches did you eat while you were there?"

What a stupid question, she thought. But an obvious one. She'd never had that flavour before or since.

"Lobster sandwiches," she said embarrassed. She hated questions that focused on her impoverished background. She wouldn't have been able to afford them at that time, and even though she could now, had no interest in eating them.

This time, when the screen went dark, Yasmeen was trying to remain patient. She'd blocked out the flames as much as she could, but smoke was getting through the door, and she was coughing.

Question 3 soon flashed up. "What was the first name of the girl you befriended there?

This question needed even less time to answer. They'd been best friends for several months. "Amara. Her name was Amara." She wanted to shout but her voice wasn't carrying. She told herself it was the smoke, but really, she felt uncomfortable saying her name. It had been so long since she said it. But she wasn't exactly in a great bargaining position.

She looked away from the screen, though she heard the swish of a new question, forcing her to look up.

"Fourth and final question. You have seven tattoos but only ever discuss six. What is the seventh tattoo, and where is it on your body?"

It was an easy answer, but she still didn't want to give it. More than the flames, this was the punishment. Forcing her to reveal something she had been desperate to keep hidden. Something she never talked about in her book, in interviews or even with any of her family, friends or lovers.

As the sound of the flames got hotter, the sense of panic left her. She'd been desperate to leave this competition since it started and now, in a way, there was a way out. What did she really have on the outside? Everyone hated her. She was sure her fan club was now mostly made up of horny teenagers and dirty old men, save for the odd woman who thought she could convert her sexuality full-time. She knew her family wouldn't miss her. Now she'd lost out on the millions, her fans probably wouldn't last long. There was always a trendy new influencer, complete with hip slang, more current music references and an even greater understanding of technology. Would it really be so bad if she just lay here?

The smoke would do the damage. She knew enough about fires to know smoke inhalation was a huge cause. She wanted to be cremated anyway. She wasn't really that bothered by what happened to her body after she was dead.

The only person she'd really cared about was Amara. And she knew the details of the day they met as well as anything.

It was in early April. She remembered as she had tried reading *Nineteen Eighty-Four* on her way to the competition. She'd grabbed it off of her mother's bookshelf. It was a long book, and she hadn't finished it, but she did love that opening line. "It was a bright cold day in April, and the clocks were striking thirteen." The fact it was sunny when she had started reading it made her smile.

Wait a second, she said to herself. The invite had said Saturday the 14th, but it had been changed to the Sunday. She'd only found out because she'd overheard someone from her school saying that now they'd changed the day, they wouldn't be able to go able to go. The girl had so many fliers telling her of the change of date, yet in Yasmeen's neighbourhood there hadn't been any.

Yasmeen had felt second-class even before she turned up, but it was worse when she arrived. People looking at her as though she didn't belong. There were all the country club snobs, knowing their future was secure without needing to work for it. She had contempt for them all. They were talking about which beach resort they were going to vacation in and which designer dress they would be buying that day. After the two buses and a train to get there and the same needed to get back, she didn't even have enough for a snack. There always seemed enough money for her father's beer, she noted bitterly.

She stayed away from the cafeteria and found a quiet spot to sit in the grass outside the building. A brunette the same age as Yasmeen came up to her a few moments later and just started talking.

"Hi, I'm Amara," said the confident and chatty girl, reaching out her hand. Yasmeen didn't answer or reach hers out, but that didn't seem to put off this friendly stranger. "I know what you're thinking. Amara, right?" she continued, as she arranged her ponytail. "It means Everlasting. My parents got quite spiritual when they had me. They weren't when they first got together. My older brothers are called Horatio and Tarquin." With that, she laughed and started sharing randomly quirky details about her family. In spite of herself, Yasmeen found herself charmed.

"Have you eaten yet?" asked Amara politely, as she reached into her bag. Yasmeen watched astounded as Amara picked out a carefully prepared lunch, which included lobster sandwiches and caviar finger food. Noticing that Yasmeen's bag was empty, Amara paused only for the briefest of seconds before immediately started sharing her food. "Come on, we can split it. You know, I almost forgot mine, too. It was such a mad rush this morning."

Yasmeen was hesitant but Amara wasn't taking no for an answer. "I'm not eating alone. Besides, I'm far too nervous to finish it all, anyway."

As it turned out, neither of them made the final. They were out first round, and Amara was too embarrassed to message her mother to pick her up earlier. So instead, they talked about art, boys, family expectation, their dreams of going to Japan and Pilates. Amara had really embraced it as a way of dealing with her family's crushing expectations and explained just how much of a difference it had made. That conversation really was the happiest moment of Yasmeen's life.

It didn't end there. Over the next few months, they went to all the touristy places. Disneyland and its nearby spinoff locations, Universal Studios, the Dali Museum, the Aquarium, Legoland and the Hemingway Museum. Not to mention various restaurants and bars, including one where they did a karaoke duet. Whenever Yasmeen felt embarrassed about not paying for anything, Amara couldn't have been any nicer. "Trust me, my parents are loaded," she said with a grin. "And it's nice to be outside of the house. Tarquin's decided to rebel against our parents by playing the trumpet. It'd be bad enough if he were good. It is an improvement on ventriloquism though. Thankfully he gave that up after a month."

Yasmeen never realised she could be this happy. She would wake up with a smile on her face and actually look forward to the day ahead. It was like she had discovered a new colour; everything just felt more real. They would speak regularly on the phone and spend most of the weekend together.

When it was Amara's birthday, Yasmeen knew she had to get her something. But what do you get for someone who could afford everything you could think of? The only thing that seemed appropriate was a stuffed elephant. They had gone to a fair and despite spending what seemed like the GDP of a developing country, had been unable to win one. Yasmeen had saved up for weeks to buy one she'd seen in a store.

Yasmeen had known that Amara's house would be big. Amara had always been careful to ensure they met at the event itself, but Yasmeen was curious to see if she really did live in a mansion. Her mother had warned her not to go. "I know it's her birthday, but it's a bad idea. Like I told you before, you and her live in different worlds. She'd understand if you don't go."

What did her mother know? The teenage Yasmeen told herself, swearing loudly after she'd slammed the door. Yasmeen wasn't sure if her mother heard her and didn't particularly care. All that mattered was that she had the elephant, and Amara was going to love it. It wasn't big or that expensive, but its bright orange fur, floppy ears and long, goofy trunk meant it was certainly distinctive.

Yasmeen had guessed that Amara would live somewhere lavish and extravagant but even so, she was shocked when she saw it. It was bigger than the block she lived on. There was every type and shade of luxury car, gleaming in the sunshine so much it was like they'd been bought yesterday. And there was no avoiding the expensive jewellery, perfectly styled hair and pretty dresses.

Yasmeen was out of place, and there was no hiding from it. She was embarrassed and more than a little resentful. Those kids hadn't earned it. Why couldn't she have been brought up in a place like this? She looked at her own faded jeans, simple white blouse and ordinary charm bracelet and frowned. There really was no hiding her poverty.

Yasmeen was going to leave her present with the butler, whose accent was so posh he may as well have been speaking a different language. She didn't want to give her mother the satisfaction of being proved right, so she'd sit at the train station for a few hours while finishing the book on Pilates she had just started reading.

But she heard a squeal, and before she could say anything, was being hugged tighter than she had ever been before. "I'm so glad you came!" Amara's smile only got wider when she saw the present.

"Oh, you didn't have to get me anything!" said the birthday girl, who had already had plenty of practice receiving presents that day. Before

Yasmeen could say anything, Amara had ripped off the carefully wrapped gift, saying, "Oh, I know I should wait, but..."

She didn't finish the sentence, and there was a long pause while she just stared at the fluffy stuffed toy. Yasmeen wondered if she was disappointed. Though it had cost her a fortune, she wouldn't have been surprised if Amara's other guests had gifted her a tropical island or a rare bird. How could she compete with that?

"It's perfect," said Amara in a soft, quiet voice that Yasmeen had never heard her use before. Yasmeen couldn't believe how much her best friend, maybe only real friend, loved her present and how happy that made her. And to think she'd have missed it if she'd left it with the butler.

"I'm going to name him Bing Bong!" Amara grinned and immediately got the two of them to pose for a photo with Bing Bong in the middle. Despite Amara's love of spirituality and embracing of Eastern cultures, at times she really was just a big kid who had seen every Disney film at least three times, including *Inside Out*.

"Come on, I want you to meet everyone," said Amara as she introduced her to what seemed like 300 people while still holding onto Bing Bong. After a while, it became hard to distinguish which rich kid was which. But that didn't stop the warmth with which Amara introduced her. Some she even showed photos of them together or tried to explain some of their inside jokes.

The fact they didn't understand any of them made Yasmeen treasure the friendship even more. They had their own secret club, and whether anyone wanted in or not didn't matter. They could be an army of two. That was enough.

At that point, someone new arrived. Even if she hadn't heard the doorbell, she would have known from the sense of activity. There was a collective gasp from the girls who were there. It was like a movie star had turned up. People reached for their phones, desperate to ensure they were the first ones to see this special guest emerge. It all seemed rather ridiculous. Why were all these people, who already had more money than God, in thrall to one person?

And then she saw him get out of the car. He was the most handsome man she had ever seen in her life. She had no idea someone could be that good-looking. He belonged in a film or on stage. Who was he?

"Oh, that's Willard Masterson," said Amara with a frustrated sigh. Yasmeen couldn't believe such an indifferent reaction to such a beautiful human being. If she had known someone like him, she would want everyone to know.

"He's such a jerk," said Amara with a hint of bitterness, turning away and walking back to the drinks section. "We were dating last year, but I caught him with another girl. I didn't even invite him today. I don't know why he's here." She shook her head. "My father and his father do business together. I bet he's behind it."

Yasmeen had to force herself to look away. Was she going mad, or had he noticed her? Even with all these swooning females, she could have sworn he looked at her and smiled. It couldn't be. No way such a wealthy, handsome, stylish guy like him would notice someone like her. She didn't belong. Yet, she knew he had looked at her.

Amara was determined not to let her mood change by Willard's arrival. It became impossible to stick close to her though. People kept handing her gifts, large and heavy and wrapped professionally. Amara was apologetic, but Yasmeen was happy to let her have her moment. It wasn't for her to hog the birthday girl.

Yasmeen was curious to try the cakes and snacks. She had never seen such decadence. She didn't even know how to eat some of the things on the trays and had to look around to see how others were doing it. Despite this, she could see some of the girls sniggering. Maybe they were laughing at her tatty clothes and not her table manners. Either way, it hurt.

Without Amara, there was no shield. It was time for Yasmeen to say goodbye. The party had gone well. Amara had loved the gift. Yasmeen had seen how joyful Amara was, but it was still a reminder of how their worlds were so very different. What was Yasmeen going to do when it was her birthday in a month? How could she compete with this? The longer she stayed, the more bitter she would become. It took every bit of willpower not to go over there and shove some cake in their faces and rip their frilly little dresses.

"Don't mind them, they're just jealous," said a voice so confident, so vibrant she knew who it was before she even turned around. Could a voice be dashing? If it could, his was.

And she should have left it there. When Yasmeen still replayed that scene years later, she wondered what she could have done instead. Shove cake in his face. Throw water on his shirt. Shout out to Amara. Instead, she did nothing.

"I don't think we've met," said the gorgeous stranger with a smile so gleaming it looked as though his teeth had been polished with diamonds. "I'm Willard."

She was torn between looking at him, not looking at him and not looking at all the other girls whose jealous hatred made her smile. All the money they had, and they still wanted to be her right now.

"I'm Yasmeen," was the nervous reply. She wanted to be fun and interesting, but she couldn't think of anything smart or brilliant to say. So, she decided to keep her mouth shut and just smile and nod. But she remembered how Amara felt, and her sense of loyalty took over. "I can't talk to you. You cheated on Amara, and she is my best friend."

She went to leave but, a hand grabbed her arm. She actually felt her body tighten. He was so muscular, and she felt a surge of electricity just from his touch.

"Just hear me out," he said in a voice full of angelic charm. "I tried to explain this to her, but she wouldn't listen. This girl, Carly, made a move on me. You don't know what it's like. They just throw themselves at me. They think just because I am nice to them that they can force themselves on me. You can't imagine how it is. I can't go anywhere. People stare at me all the time. You don't know what it's like to be different to the idea people have about you. To be seen one way just because they don't want to get to know the real you."

"People stare at me, too, and misunderstand me, too," she'd said with a sad smile. "But you still have to be persistent. All you had to do was push her away."

"I did, but at that moment, Amara walked in. Carly set it all up. She was jealous I hadn't wanted to go out with her. But here, I'll demonstrate that it's actually hard because I can see you don't believe me."

And with that, he kissed her. Yasmeen had kissed before, but it had always felt functional. The guy would always use too much tongue or not enough. He would go too frenzied or too passive. This felt like one of those kisses her older friends had told her about. She forgot where she was in that moment and just who she was with and soon realised she was kissing him back.

And if that happened in slow motion, the rest happened as though in fast-forward. As he then leaned away, she saw Amara with her face like thunder. Yasmeen had no idea a stuffed toy could be ripped apart so easily, but Amara threw Bing Bong's head and then the rest of the furry elephant before storming off. Willard winked at Yasmeen and then walked off with a smirk.

Despite leaving 15 voicemails and coming back to the house three times, her best friend never responded. She didn't think she could feel any worse, until three days later in the newspaper, when she saw that Amara hadn't been paying enough attention when crossing the road and was hit by a passing truck. She was killed instantly.

Yasmeen still didn't know how she got through that period. To go from complete joy to utter devastation was worse than any hell of any afterlife. She spent a great deal of time wondering whether to go to the funeral. After a lot of internal debate covering several days, Yasmeen decided to go, only to be stopped at the door and told she would not be let in under any circumstances.

Of all the mistakes she had made in her life, kissing that manipulative twerp was the one she was most ashamed of. And it was one she'd intended to take to her grave.

She took off her left sock, lifted her foot and showed a furry elephant tattoo to the camera, wiping away a tear. "It's an elephant to remember Amara. She was my best friend, and I miss her."

With that, a loud noise sounded. The sounds of the flames disappeared, the temperature was put back to normal and the wall came down. It turns out they had recreated her apartment, helped by some hard-working set designers. The fact they could use a lot of the items she already had, plus the fact her apartment wasn't that big to begin with, had made it more straightforward. The street itself didn't need much detail as the actual lighting was so poor it wasn't like they had to build a whole block. The heat had been controlled through specialist machines and the flames through visual effects, something that had been made very aware to viewers before the challenge had started.

It took a while for Yasmeen to realise what had happened. She had gone through a whole host of emotions and a few moments before had been quite happy to wait for death. Now, she was alive, and she really wasn't sure what to think. It should be a good thing and yet it didn't feel like it. All the raw emotions she had repressed for so long would have to be dealt with.

She didn't immediately notice the "Challenge completed" lights and completely missed the betting figures. The results only showed that people really didn't know what to make of the rebellious Pilates influencer with more sensitivity than they realised.

"Yasmeen reveals the reason for her seventh tattoo: 28.2%"
"Yasmeen fails to reveal the reason for her seventh tattoo: 71.8%"

When she did, she found she had no emotion left to react. She didn't have the energy to think about the audience being right or wrong, let alone move. It was everything just exploding together. That she'd participated. That she'd failed. That she had come so close. That she'd got to know five strangers and would probably never see any of them again. That their fates would still be lumped in together. That she had to reveal a long-held secret to the whole world. That she had no idea how everyone she knew would react. And that she had no idea what to do now. She was lost and alone.

That's when an arm reached up to lift her up. She was too exhausted to even look to see who it was, though she knew enough to know it wasn't Selina or one of the security guards. After finally getting to her feet, she glanced up to see who it was and was astonished. Yasmeen hadn't seen him in a long time, but she knew who he was immediately.

It was Tarquin, Amara's brother. She had only seen him once, when he had told her in no uncertain terms that she was not welcome at the funeral and had to leave. Amara had always described him as a bit of a dreamer, a poet and a goofball. But on that that cold, wet, blistery September morning, he was bitter, resentful, angry and judgemental, blaming her for making Amara so distracted from lack of sleep that she couldn't even cross a road.

All these years later, he looked at her expressionless. Yasmeen stared at him for clues of what he was thinking. Why was he here, and what did he want? She stared at him, and he stared at her just as intently before his face broke into a sad smile.

"We should have let you come to the funeral." He paused a long time. She saw that the subsequent years had been tough on him. She'd never considered what he had gone through or whether he had regretted his outburst. She hadn't thought of him at all. Just Amara and what could have been.

The 29-year-old, who momentarily rekindled a youthful gaze on his weathered face, looked at the floor in shy discomfort. "Others wanted you to come, but I couldn't face it. I blamed you for it, which I know was wrong. And I said some horrible things, which was worse."

Tarquin had thought about that day a lot and his behaviour, which had been so out of character. At various times over the years, he had picked up the phone or drafted an email before changing his mind. He never knew what to say or whether she wanted to hear from him.

He forced himself to look away from the floor and up at her face. If he wanted an instant reaction, he wasn't going to get one. Yasmeen's face was impossible to read. Feeling uncomfortable, he fumbled in his pockets before bringing out a scrap of paper and handing it to her in a way that couldn't be seen by the cameras. "That's where I am staying for the next few days. If you want to talk or have any questions, I'll be there until next Tuesday. If you don't, I'll completely understand."

And with that, he hurried awkwardly to the exit. Yasmeen stood there, still shocked at his appearance and his apology.

In the time that Yasmeen stood there after he had left, it was again clear just how different both commentaries were. While the psychiatrist Denis Kavolkan discussed the effect trauma can have and how there can be different remedies and exercises to help relieve the pain to his small but loyal following, the zany duo and their pop culture references were going in a completely different direction. While guessing whether the "Pilates Ramones girl" would "kiss him, kick him or kill him", their emphasis was on famous "walks" and exits, with references to everything from John Cleese, Aerosmith and Run DMC, *The Usual Suspects*, *The Third Man* and Johnny Cash.

After a few moments, Yasmeen calmly composed herself, stood up straight and walked out of the room with a great sense of purpose. While watching Yasmeen pick up her phone and other items, viewers were desperate for clues as to whether she had forgiven Tarquin or whether she was getting ready for revenge. Much to their disappointment, the rebellious and yet misunderstood influencer wasn't giving anything away.

Finale

While all this was going on, Madison was back in the same bedroom and trying not to look at the space where Yasmeen's things had been. It had felt weird when it was just the two of them. Now, as she lay alone on her bed, looking at the ceiling and trying to stay calm, the enormity of it all was still being processed.

She remembered how she felt when she entered the competition. When she had run into ordinary people off the street, she was either ignored, mocked or angrily confronted. Now, she would be going home, and her life was looking up. Without even thinking about it, there were three reasons to be joyous.

The first was obvious. Money. Her family was always extremely wealthy, but that had always been her grandfather's money, as had been pointed out to her by any number of relatives and no shortage of journalists, rivals and bitter exes. No one ever knew the pressure of being super wealthy. People thought all her problems could be solved by writing a cheque. Now, she was going to be able to relax with a long and expensive holiday somewhere quiet. She really was shattered.

The second was avoiding the sinister-sounding challenge. The fact she had no idea what the other punishment tasks had involved or what their effect had been on the other five competitors really sent shivers down her spine. She had never hidden her fear of needles, or trypanophobia to use the proper term, from those closest to her. They knew not to talk about it or even make jokes at her expense. She had no idea how heroin addicts managed. How could you willingly shove something that felt like a knife, just for some added kicks? She wondered how the other competitors had managed. If only they could swap punishments. That would still have been entertaining.

And thirdly, the restoration of her public image. Now she was the champion, she could begin the process of repairing her tattered reputation. People could see her for who she was. She wasn't the heartless snob she'd been portrayed as, just someone who had a stressful job and didn't always deal with it as well as she could have.

People forgot how much good work she'd done since joining the company. People only saw the lavish balls and glamorous dresses, but she wasn't there just to pose for photos. Not only was she on the board, she took an active role in managing European operations. That's why she had learnt French. People thought it was just to have an *Emily in Paris* experience or because she had a French-sounding surname. They didn't see the hours she had spent with private tutors, not just to learn the words and their pronunciation but also to better understand French culture and how best to do business there. It had worked. The move into the French market had been a huge success, and further growth was now planned into other French-speaking territories.

As well as being responsible for major company decisions, she took charge of several major corporate events throughout the year. She chose the overall theme, selected the DJs or musicians, carefully filtered the seating chart and decided which caterers to use and which press to invite. In her life, she had only really made a few mistakes. The other five were bound to have made far more. The producers of the show probably just wanted someone a little different to the others.

While some members of the family had branded her a disgrace to the family name after her few public errors of judgement, others had been supportive, as had a close circle of friends. Not as wide a circle as she hoped, but still strong enough.

Which was a question that had been bothering her. If she had won, which she knew she had, where was her trophy? Why couldn't she see her family? Why couldn't she communicate with the world? The madness was over and yet, it still continued. And she was still being filmed.

As though reading her mind, the doors swung open, and she saw people she hadn't seen in too long. Her two brothers came in first, followed by some cousins and her closest friends. Her aunts and uncles were noticeably absent. As were her parents.

But the ones that were there hugged her so tightly that she could barely breathe. They were carrying champagne, balloons and celebratory banners. "Winner", "Champion" and "Congratulations Madison" were some of the more obvious ones, but there were so many she was losing track. The music came on loud, a makeshift dancefloor was set up and before she knew it, the party was rocking.

The fact that Madison just wanted to sleep was forgotten by all. She was being congratulated by everyone and was trying her best not to look uncomfortable. Because she was so glamorous and stylish, people assumed she loved the spotlight, being at the heart of everything. The truth was, she hated it, she always had. Even as a winner, she felt she was being punished.

Selina appeared from out of nowhere and indicated to come with her somewhere quieter and away from the cameras. The influential TV executive relaxed her tense expression and reached out her hand. "I know you detest this sort of scene, but your family and friends really wanted to celebrate you. I held them off for an hour, but they would have killed all the security guards if we'd kept them in any longer. As big as they are, they wouldn't have stood a chance against your lot."

Was that a smile? Madison had never seen this lighter side of Selina and wasn't sure what to say. It was actually creeping her out. It unnerved her until she told herself that there must have been a huge amount of stress in organising such an ambitious project, but now the show was finished, they could all relax. It was all over. All Madison had to do was keep that smile on her face for a little longer and then she could do whatever she wanted.

"There is one thing for you to know," said Selina with that same smile. "You will have to go back out there. We're going to present the $7.2 million in front of the studio. There will be a trophy, too."

"Will Buck host it?" Madison answered quicker than she intended.

Selina pretended not to know that the two had never got on. "He's been our host throughout. Why wouldn't he?" Selina looked intently at Madison, almost challenging her to take her dislike further. "You should see the fan mail he gets. He's done great promotion on the show, too. He's a huge reason the show has been the success it's been."

"So, you're surprised that a show putting six people through hell did well in the ratings?" said Madison more bitterly than she intended. Whether it was the fact she had to be in front of the audience again, her being exhausted from trying to answer all the same questions from those closest to her for the past hour, or whether it was hearing Buck get so much praise, she really had snapped.

Selina glared at her and took a few seconds to compose herself before replying. "It wasn't me who humiliated that tramp or berated that fast-food checkout girl. It wasn't me who, for all her talk of being a feminist, forgot to be a human being when your friend's husband came to you for help. And it certainly wasn't me who bullied her employees or mocked her neighbours and then acted surprised when no one spoke up for you."

Seeing that Madison had gone quiet, she decided to hammer home the point in a softer tone. "I'm familiar with the agencies you were desperate to represent you. I saw their notes. Trust me, you were finished. You have a lot of good qualities, but the public wasn't interested in seeing any of them. All you have to do is play nice for just a little longer. Trust me, the other five would kill to be where you are right now. If you want to be grateful, you're welcome. If not, I really couldn't care less."

Madison went to say something, but Selina had gone. Madison knew it was stupid to make someone so powerful that angry, but she couldn't stop herself. Even being the champion, Madison still wasn't happy. The business part of her brain couldn't understand why she wasn't more grateful or smarter about not offending someone incredibly influential.

Madison took a glass of wine and decided to join the rest of the party and relax. If everyone else was having fun, she would do her best to do the same. She'd won this incredibly difficult competition. She should celebrate, damn it! It was great to see all her friends so happy. She had so much she wanted to know about the outside world, but being filmed, she knew it could all wait until later.

But when she saw Selina again hours later, she froze. Something was different about her. It wasn't just the fact that her outfit was now all black: there was a steely determination to her.

Selina tapped her champagne glass: "Thank you everyone for coming. I'm glad you've all enjoyed the party. It's now time for the ceremony."

The powerful TV executive walked towards the studio with such authority everyone followed her, even though most people wanted to stay. It was just going to be an ordinary trophy lift, quick photo, short speech, and they just wanted to carry on drinking and dancing. A few sighed, but only after they knew Selina was out of earshot.

As Madison walked towards the studio, she couldn't shake the feeling that something was off. There was nothing she could put her finger on, just a sense that there was one final surprise in store. Her mood wasn't helped by seeing Buck in a shiny new suit as soon as she entered the studio This time, it was silver, with a gold collar and sleeves.

"Welcome back, you glorious, wonderful, magnificent people," bellowed Buck, shaking her out of her inner thoughts. "You've now seen the five challenges. They were quite something, weren't they! And that means that now we have our winner. Madison Larouch, take a bow. You have won the greatest show on TV! How does it feel?"

Madison had never won a trophy before and was caught off guard by how happy that made her. She was never into sports, and her private school focused little on grades. Although she'd taken school seriously, she knew how much influence her grandfather had behind the scenes and how disposable the teachers were.

"I'm so happy. I really am. I just want to thank all the people who've been rooting for me since I came on the show. It's meant a lot to know I've had supporters. People who know I've made some mistakes along the way, who know I'm a good person. They believe in me, and I won't let you down."

It wasn't quite as eloquent a speech as she had imagined, but then, she was exhausted and just a little drunk. Under the circumstances, it was pretty solid. No goading, short and classy. She wasn't sure how much of it she really meant, but that wasn't important right now.

From the way he held the microphone, Buck had expected more. "Not quite Shakespeare, was it, people? But it's all good, you know we forgive her. She's been through a lot. Not as much as the other five if you think about it, but she is the last one standing, and that's quite the achievement. Congratulations to our new Queen of Spin."

There was a generous round of applause, and Buck made sure to lead it, with the cameras capturing his megawatt smile.

"To those either in the studio or at home, or wherever you are right now, you've been with us every step of the way." Buck spoke as though on an election drive before he broke into that inescapable grin. "And those who showed up late, hey, we're good. You joined in time because we've got one extra shock for you to enjoy."

There were genuine gasps from the audience, which Selina noted with a grin. People had obviously thought the show was going to fade into the distance like a polite substitute teacher handing back the reins. They really had learned nothing about what *Wheel of Phobia* was about.

"We've had so many shocks along the way, you didn't just think we were going to finish it all with a simple trophy lift, did you?" said Buck, incredulous, and laughed that infectious laugh of his. Madison just thought it was toxic. Like one of those ancient kings who would laugh just before he had a court jester put down.

At that moment, Madison's trophy and envelope were taken away from her, and she was sat down on a chair. Madison looked over to Selina, who had a look in her eye that Madison immediately knew was suspicious. This wasn't going to be some cameo from Buck's family. This was bad. The question was, how bad?

"The money and trophy are still yours," Buck assured her. "We're just going to have a little fun first. Well, it will be fun for us, anyhow. We'll soon see how you find it," and then laughed again.

"First off, why don't you share with people what your phobia is?"

"I'd rather not," said Madison annoyed.

"Ah, Madison, you must know there are no secrets here," Buck said with gusto. "No worries, I'll tell them. It's trypanophobia."

The Manhattan native hated revealing personal things about herself and even more, having them revealed for her. Madison vowed revenge on everyone in this show. She didn't care how confident or well-connected Selina was. She was going down. But now, it was about controlling that anger, even if the audience obviously had no idea what the phobia was.

"It's better known as the fear of needles," explained a miked-up Selina to the crowd, though she stayed within the shadows. "It is a common one. At some level, it affects up to 10% of the world's population."

"Well, you'd have liked the challenge a lot less than the other 90%," smirked Buck as he then looked at Selina. "Let me tell them what it was. I'm going to tell them."

Buck was like a little kid begging for permission. Selina nodded.

"It was amazing. You would have had five crossbows facing different parts of your body, but you would have been able to change the direction with the help of journalists and influencers you've interacted with over the years. As an added twist they would be blindfolded. Would they have helped you or "accidentally" aimed the needles someplace more painful? That was the question!"

There were gasps from the audience. It was clear they would have loved to have seen that. But Buck wasn't going to allow their disappointment to ruin the evening. He saw himself as a king of current comedy, a prince of popularity and an emperor of entertainment. This was his show, and he was just teasing them, changing the energy before he ramped it back up.

"That just shows how incredible all the challenges were." His voice was even louder to remind them who was in charge. "But that's why we're bringing you this extra surprise."

Madison then felt something touch her skin and with a shock, realised that she was now connected to something electronic. With a sunken feeling, she realised what it was. It was a lie detector test. And not just a fell-off-the-back-of-a-truck kind of lie detector test. This wasn't merely some technology where you only focused on a few squiggly lines. This was a state-of-the-art invention, where she felt exposed, physically and emotionally.

Every aspect of her face and every facet of her voice could be viewed by everyone. Every last blink, every last twitch, every last pause. Different cameras were focused on all parts of her face and complex audio technology to capture the sound of her voice, showing up on big screens in the studio and for those watching back home. There was no place for her to hide.

As a set of carefully organised graphics came up, an intellectual-sounding voice on the loudspeakers explained just why this was the most impressive set of lie detector tests ever invented. Most people ignored the explanation of molecules, heart rate, eye sensory movement, pulse irregularities and brain activity to instead focus on Madison's panicked reaction.

Madison had made sure she would control her emotions, especially on camera. But for the first time, she was really struggling. She was a private person, and this would go against everything she was, everything she believed in.

She thought back to the contract her agent had pleaded with her to sign. Surely there had to be something that forbade it. Some loophole. She had won. What extra could there be? But one look at Selina showed that Madison was completely powerless and would just try and keep control as best as she could. If only it were that simple.

"Wait a second, this can't be right?" she screamed. "This wasn't in the contract!"

"It most certainly was," said a still-hidden Selina, and the cameras panned to a highlighted verse in a very convoluted-looking block of text. Experts would later marvel at the use of language and how brilliantly a point could be made disguised in a vague, longer sentence. But in the short term, that meant she could be controlled like a celebrity puppet.

"What's to stop me leaving right now? You can't stop me!"

Madison got up, but several security guards came towards her. Selina's voice kept the same composed manner she had throughout the series. "Ah, but we can. The same contract that meant you couldn't leave before the challenges had finished applies just as much here. This is just the final flourish. If you break the terms of that, you'd have to do the challenge just described and lose the money and trophy. We have the crossbows in the next room. It wouldn't be hard to set up. The five who'd be in charge of the crossbow are currently enjoying a free bar on the floor above."

Five drunks in charge of crossbow-filled needles, who may not even be fans of hers to begin with, was an even worse situation than this one, shuddered Madison. She hadn't thought there could be anything worse than a public lie detector.

"Well, people, we have our final scene," said Buck majestically. "You watched the main performance, now let's enjoy an encore!"

He soaked in the drama of the moment, even if the crowd was slightly quieter tonight.

"Before we go ahead, Madison will be happy to know there won't be any questions on anything sexual, religious or political. I was outvoted. I'm kidding, I'm kidding! And nothing that will reveal anything private about her family or friends. Hey, we play fair."

Madison scoffed, which Buck only used as fuel.

"Trust me, we could have gone a lot worse. I've seen that contract. Gave me a headache, I can tell you that. But it's all legit. I had a whole set of questions ready. They were great. But I don't count as an audience. I'd be an amazing audience. I'd be just as pumped as you all are right now."

Buck suddenly turned back to face Madison and asked with a confident innocence, "Anything you want to say before we start?"

Madison had a thousand questions and yet all she could muster was one. "Why are you doing this?"

For the first time, Buck actually took a long time to say something. People had never seen him so composed and reflective. "Well, I'm the one asking the questions, but hey, I'll answer you," he answered in an unusually serious tone. "I think it's fun. You've had a lot of fun at different points in your life at other people's expense, and now we're going to have some. You always made it clear you were in control, now we have it. And as we have it for a little longer, let's learn something about you. That's just my answer, though. It's probably different for other folks."

Madison stared directly at the camera. "I think this is unjust, unfair and shameful," said Madison.

"Wait a second," said Buck with a smirk. "Don't those words mean pretty much the same thing? I may not have a fancy education like you, but I know that's quite the repetition. What's the technical word for saying something more than necessary in a sentence?"

Someone in the audience shouted "Tautology," and Buck grinned. "Thanks, buddy. Good to know."

A bucket of popcorn was then brought to him with great fanfare as the showman aspect of his personality returned. "In fact, I'm going to watch it myself in a comfortable seat backstage. Like the scene after the credits in a superhero film. I'm going to leave you fine audience in the capable hands of someone you might recognise. Maybe not his appearance, but definitely his voice."

And with a smile, Buck started eating the popcorn and walking off stage, getting the last word over Madison as usual. He shook hands with Eric Cho, the podcaster from before who was now going to take his place. Selina loved the energy of Buck but knew he would not be good as a traditional interviewer, especially as he clearly didn't like Madison.

Eric soon walked into the main part of the studio with a smile that he hoped hid how nervous he was. He had been shocked to get the call the night after the interview and had crammed knowledge relating to any possible questions that he may need to ask. His husband watched on supportively and grabbed his hand as a form of reassurance. Eric smiled in gratitude.

Timed for Eric's arrival, a transparent but expensive glass electronic cylinder bowl with different balls inside was brought right next to Madison. "You'll also get to choose the four questions," said Eric. "Once you've chosen, you can't change it. If you read out anything different on the card, we'll know, so don't do that."

Madison wanted to say something, but she knew she was powerless now. The contract would have held up. She knew there was no way they would have her here like this if they weren't bulletproof legally. She knew she was on camera, she knew she had to protect the family name. All she could do now was stay composed.

Without any fanfare, Eric indicated for her to start. Selina watched on intently from the side.

After a long breath, Madison picked up the first one. The earlier she started, the quicker it would all be over. "Why does Desmond Stanleys dislike you?"

She winced as she read out the card, something picked up on all the cameras as well as the change in her heart rate. Desmond was someone who she had never liked. He had all the right qualifications on paper, but he had such a nervous disposition. He could never make his points without doubting himself or giving a big disclaimer. "It might just be me...", "Sorry if the point has already been made...", "If you don't mind explaining it to someone who had a simpler education like me..." It was exhausting.

Although she had read every useful book on leadership, Madison hated firing people. She didn't mind the human element of it. She wasn't firing kids. She was removing useless adults and saw it as doing them a favour. But it was expensive, an admittance of a bad decision and a nuisance to sort out the paperwork. So, she made a vow to ensure she did just enough to make him quit but not enough that he would have a good case in court. It was rather brilliant. So much so, he had left in two months rather than the six she had planned.

"I don't know Desmond too well. He used to work under me. He was at the company before I joined and left about a year after I joined. As for why he wouldn't like me, he wasn't that good an employee. I wasn't surprised when he left."

"He'd been there 11 years. He can't have been that bad?"

"I get paid to make big decisions," explained his former boss. "I'm sure he did fine after."

"That isn't quite true," said a voice suddenly, and she didn't need to look up to see who it was. "I was a good employee. It took me a long time to recover from the constant bullying and immense gaslighting you did in those two months. After I left, I was a wreck. I struggled to sleep and got addicted to pills. That got me fired from my next two jobs, almost cost me my marriage, and ravaged my savings. I'm back on track now, no thanks to you. Working under you was the worst experience of my life and nearly destroyed me!"

Madison may have been quiet before, but she wasn't going to take this one lying down. "Your life after you left the company is not my concern. While I wished you well, you made bad decisions and suffered consequences."

"Madison, just before you do say anything further, I'll let you in on something," Eric said with a calm steeliness as he handed her a heavy document from his briefcase. "There's a very detailed document that covers your behaviour towards him in those two months. As well as the experiences of other employees who left abruptly within the same three-year period. I suggest you look at it, with whoever you choose to share it with, before deciding how to respond. If the allegations are true, I would suggest you consider aspects of your leadership moving forward."

Madison paused, surprised by this level-headed attitude by the interviewer. The behaviour discussed in the document must be pretty serious. It was just business. She hadn't seen anything wrong with the way she had treated them, but she knew she was going to have to read it all carefully. Maybe the business world was changing.

That had been a tough one to start with. Maybe it was going to get easier. She reached into the cylinder and read out a second ball. "Why didn't you listen to Henry Courtauld when he came to you for help?"

The cameras captured Madison's discomfort. Unlike Desmond's case, the name was already known to most of the people in the audience. Madison was still going to fight this one, though.

"Henry was married to a close friend. My loyalty was with her, not Henry."

At that moment, several photos of Madison with Henry were shown on the screen. Although there wasn't a romantic element, it was clear there was a genuine bond between the two.

"Do you regret anything?" probed Eric.

Madison breathed in heavily. "I don't do regrets. It's easy to look at things differently now, but at the time, I did what I thought was best."

"For those unfamiliar with the case, Madison's friend Francesca went on to be convicted of domestic abuse," Eric explained. "Over the course of several years, she stole from him, physically assaulted him and belittled him in front of his friends. She would also hide his keys, take bank cards out of his wallet without telling him and move books around in his study.

When he told you what was happening and came to you for help, what did you say?"

Madison went quiet.

"We have listened to the audio he left you when he was genuinely distressed," said Eric, looking down at his notes. "We won't play it back to you now, in respect for his family, who are still at the clinic where he is getting treatment. He has been allowed out a few times, but he suffered a setback recently. We will, though, play the audio you left for him. A copy was made before you deleted it."

"Grow up, you big baby!" came Madison's taunting voice through the loudspeaker. "Complaining because you think your wife is being mean to you. Man up, will you! Honestly, you need to sort yourself out. Come to me when you have some proper adult problems and you've taken off your diaper! You're an absolute joke!" Her laughter could be heard before she abruptly ended the call.

There wasn't much more to say to that. Madison hadn't heard that voicemail since she made it, not even when she deleted it. She hadn't realised she had been that cruel. She went to say something, but the words didn't come out.

Eric didn't say anything, but after a while gently nudged the expensive cylinder bowl for the third question.

"What was the Reginald Dyer incident about?" read out Madison in a detached voice.

That was the one that had set everything off. The one where all the hatred towards her had started. The incident that changed her life into Before and After. She realised bitterly that he was the reason she was here at all.

The thing that was all forgotten about, of course, was that she had actually gone out to the homeless guy with some food from her event. She thought that rather than just call the police or get her security to deal with the guy who had been hassling guests at the gates, it would be more humane to give him something before asking him to move on. If there was a photographer or a bystander to capture that moment, even better.

But he didn't stop complaining. For a guy with barely any teeth and a posture that made him look like a human question mark, he sure had a lot of attitude. He didn't like the fact that she had only brought one type of sandwich, and it was not enough and then no water. And "Why no napkins? Do you see a sink?" He was so bitter and judgemental.

She was not used to being spoken to like that.

When her friend came round to see why she was taking so long, she snapped. She couldn't be seen losing out to sewer scum.

"Do you have any idea how much I'm worth?" she had said, grabbing the champagne glass out of her hand and pouring it down his scraggly hair. She hadn't got anywhere in life by allowing herself to be pushed around. She could easily have mocked his appearance, but she was a classy lady. She didn't want to make it personal.

Of course, the pictures of her pouring expensive champagne over his head made her look like a heartless snob. An heiress humiliating an elderly tramp wasn't exactly the photoshoot her marketing team had in mind. So, it seemed a good idea to blame the outburst on a reaction to some sexist comments. After all, who wouldn't get angry when hearing a comment that a woman should be in the kitchen, not a boardroom? It was a brilliant idea. Turn defence into attack. People were bound to believe her and not the guy who counted a doorway or a bench as a home.

Only, it was more complicated. It turns out there was a video of the whole interaction filmed by an aspiring filmmaker. Unhelpfully, it only showed her and didn't show any of the patronising faces the homeless guy had pulled throughout her conversation. Without his silly smirks, all of what he said sounded quite reasonable. Like a diner at a restaurant asking for extra ketchup or a Coke without ice. And rather than come across as nasty, he just seemed like a cheeky old uncle rather than the outdated sexist he had been accused of. The fact she had accused him of it when it had never happened made a lot of people uncomfortable.

And then deciding to humiliate him, not least when the wealth she had bragged about had come from her grandfather, only worsened it.

If she thought the story could be buried, she was wrong. There was some mockery at her expense, but it was mostly outrage and some very sobering statistics about poverty. That over 653,000 people in the US had experienced homelessness in the past year, a 12% increase from the previous year. That first-time homelessness had risen 23%. That half of homeless individuals were unsheltered. And then there were sobering details on minorities and children and how shelters were closing. Not to mention all kinds of worrying stories told by those who were struggling to stay warm, fed and safe. The fact that the tramp she had humiliated had once served in the army and heroically toured in Afghanistan made her seem a coward and a spoilt brat.

It only got worse.

A hard-hitting journalist wrote a scathing article entitled "Toxic Feminity: The Hypocrite in High Heels". The report revealed her "bumper sticker sisterhood" was all talk, as she had only employed two women out of her nine hires. Not to mention having made several of the women cry, humiliated a popular long-serving female VP who stood up to her in a meeting and made it harder to work flexible hours, severely impacting the mothers in the workforce. It didn't mention the fact that she had tried the softer approach with them, but they had started to abuse her kindness, so she had to get tougher.

Her marketing team tried everything, but her name being in the news so often helped push an agenda of why blue-chip firms couldn't help out homeless people. Why couldn't there be a law that made big companies pay a small percentage to homeless shelters? Couldn't tax breaks given to major conglomerates instead be directed towards charities looking after those most vulnerable? Could long-neglected buildings not be redesigned to house them? Of course, it was never going to happen, but that didn't stop the headlines. Any hope a small apology and a large donation would be enough was shown to be folly.

She had immediately suspected her ex-husband, Roy. The divorce had been acrimonious from the start, with all kinds of unpleasant arguments from the past seized upon and both careers analysed in fine toothcomb levels of detail. It was always going to be, with so much money involved and so many newspapers interested. Before her fall into the role of a public villain, it had been the worst time of her life. The only saving grace had been that there hadn't been any children.

But her ex-husband wasn't involved. For all his many faults, he wasn't a liar. When he got in touch through a curt message, she knew he had moved on with his life and resented seeing his name and face on the front pages of newspapers again.

The documentary filmmaker who had filmed the altercation as part of a study into how the "Invisible Ghosts" of society lived really was a holier-than-thou type. He had been close to releasing his film, and only an extremely generous donation to pay for treatment for his aunt's rare form of cancer had convinced him to change creative direction.

Madison was thinking about all this and more before she answered in a composed fashion. "As I said at the time, I lost my temper after a heavy workload. I have done a lot to help raise money for worthy causes."

"That is true," agreed Eric. "In the 11 years before you joined, eight charities were represented. In the 14 years since you joined, your company has helped 19 charities. You've also increased the number of fundraisers, healed rifts with two different newspapers who had refused to cover the event and have visited three different continents to ensure the funds allocated to the needy were being used properly."

Madison was caught off-guard by the praise. She had hated the trips but knew how valuable they were and how much good they would do.

"You have done good work, Madison. But there is a question I'm sure we all want to ask. What was your reaction when Reginald died two years later after a heart attack?

"I was sad, of course," said Madison, though the lines on the graph changed dramatically and two different noises went off.

"Come now, Madison, don't try and lie to us. Even if the machine hadn't caught you out, I'd have noticed it."

The 41-year-old Manhattanite wasn't the first one to be caught out by Eric's forceful comments, buried as they were beneath a layer of soft charm.

"Okay, I was relieved," admitted Madison. "I was always afraid he would do some interview about how terrible I was. When he died, I knew he wouldn't be able to say anything. Even after the things the company gave to him by way of apology, I was always afraid he would wake up one day having spent it all and being ungrateful. I didn't act well around him, and when he died, I knew that it would be easier to move on with my life."

The audience went quiet. It wasn't the most pleasant logic, but it was honest, and though the audience wouldn't have wanted to admit it, they may well have agreed with her.

"Okay, your last question," said Eric, as he handed down the bowl to Madison. Madison reached around and slowly picked out a new ball.

"What happened with Hannah Brickshaw?"

If the tramp incident had been high-profile, the situation with Hannah had been very different and from a far longer period ago. Madison had a faraway look in her eyes.

"I've answered the other three," she pleaded, much to Eric's unease. "Please let me choose another."

"You know I can't do that," said Eric forcefully.

Madison looked at him sadly, as it was clear from all the data as well as more traditional methods just how affected Madison was by reading what was written on the ball.

"I haven't heard that name in a long time," said Madison who for the first time looked like a little girl looking around for help.

"Why don't you tell us all more about her and the reason why her name is mentioned here?" said Eric in a slightly friendlier tone than he would have considered in normal circumstances.

"I was ten years old," replied Madison after a long pause. "At that time, I was spoiled rotten. Daddy's little girl, mummy's little princess; I wanted for nothing. It wasn't like my two brothers, one older and one younger, did badly. They got plenty of our parents' time and bank accounts. But I know my parents had both dreamed of having a girl, and that meant I got extra privileges.

"I may have been indulged at home, but at school it was worse. I took that entitlement and made the rest of the girls, at a super-elite girls' school, fall to my whim. I was a brat. I'm not proud of it. It was a long time ago, and I grew out of it, but at the time I was the worst kind of Mean Girl."

Madison sighed deeply before continuing. "Anyhow, at my prestigious school, I was the queen. Even with everyone being from wealthy families, everything revolved around me. Life was great. But one day, that changed. This new girl, Hannah Bradshaw, joined. Other girls had joined during the year before, but none had been a problem. They were irrelevant. But it was different with Hannah. Her house was bigger than mine, she was prettier, she was smarter. Before long, she was becoming popular. I wasn't thrilled, but I still had a lot of sway. I had a huge running start over her, and she'd have to go a long way to even think about challenging me.

"She started to make some pretty big progress in a short time, but things didn't come to a head until a few months later. My family had a place in Aspen, and every summer, I'd invite a big group of girls to stay. It wasn't my birthday or anything; it was just my way of rewarding the girls who had been the most loyal to me over the previous year. Five of those places were already locked in, but the other half were always open to those who had impressed me the most. It was a big deal. Well, guess whose birthday lands smack in the middle of this trip? Hannah. And she wants to do a big event to celebrate."

"Could you not have delayed this celebration by a few days, especially as it wasn't for a fixed holiday?"

"That would have been the smart thing," said Madison with a sigh. "But I was young and stupid and spoiled. So, in the end, it became a contest. I'd guarantee the latest teen sensation pop star would be there to chat to; she'd promise an even bigger singer to perform at her party. I'd mention three chocolate fountains; she'd say there'd be a celebrity chef happy to create our own chocolate. I'd talk about the fashion contest I'd be running; she'd get everyone excited over getting a runway built and getting some photographer friend of the family to help judge. I felt she was piggybacking on my ideas. I only found out after that she'd been coming up with her ideas on her own. We really were that similar.

"When it became clear my friends were going to go to her birthday rather than my ski trip, I was incensed. It would have been okay just to put it back by a week, but no, I was so angry I decided to forget it altogether. I made up some excuse that they were renovating it after a minor fire. I even got some computer experts at my father's firm to make it look as though there really had been some sort of accident and made sure everyone in the school saw it. I told everyone that to make up for it, they had given us access to the mega cabin for two weeks in the buildup to Christmas."

"Were you surprised when Hannah invited you to her party?"

"Well, it would have been awkward for her not to," answered Madison in a matter-of-fact tone. "I had invited her to my event first, which is what set everything off. And the thing was, we hadn't actually argued. Not in front of each other, at any rate. Then, with me pulling out of the race, the contest was over before anything nasty had been said. If she had not invited me, it would have looked petty. I thought at the time she just wanted to show off. Rub my face in it."

"Did you ever consider not going?" questioned Eric.

"That was the plan," said Madison. "Why did I want to go and see everyone celebrating my enemy? Having to act all sweet and nice when inside I was so angry. I'd never been that furious in my life. I just wanted to stay in bed with a tub of ice cream and my terrier Wolfie and curse everything about her. But then, my father reminded me of the family name. "We aren't losers. We are Larouchs. Go there and make sure you're top by the end of the night.""

"So, I went. I was all fake nice and sincerity. When someone asked if I was disappointed or frustrated or sad at having lost out, I just smiled and said how could I be when I was going to the party event of the season. The thing was, I had made sure the video of the fire came out before my friends officially chose Hannah's party over mine, so I went with my head held high.

"But I was there for revenge. I had thought about making up a rumour. But after I arrived and went to put my present in the room where everyone was leaving all the presents, I noticed a dress hanging. It turns out one of the maids had thought she had chosen a different dress, so rather than being part of a big reveal, it was left unattended. It was covered, but it was easy enough to move it out of the way. I knew this was the dress she had planned on wearing as I'd overheard one of the girls talk about it the week before. I remembered I had ketchup sachets I had planned to use as part of an art project. Making up something nasty was small-time and could easily be traced back to me. It would be far better to ruin her exquisite new dress.

"So, when no one was looking, I squeezed both sachets all over the expensive lace outfit. She had obviously been planning this big entrance for later, and now it was all going to be ruined. I had my revenge."

"At the last moment, did you consider not doing it?" asked Eric optimistically.

"No," replied Madison without hesitating. "I wasn't a nice person back then. My main thought was about ensuring I wouldn't get caught. That's why I hid the used sachets in one of the girls' rucksacks."

"So you framed an innocent child and ruined an expensive dress of a girl who had been planning her birthday for weeks?" clarified Eric.

There was a long sigh as Madison grew paler and fidgeted with her hands. "I imagine you've done a lot of research. You know that's not the worst part of the story."

"It's important to let everyone know the context of what happened," insisted Eric.

Madison nodded in a wistful way before continuing. "So anyway, when Hannah removes the cover and discovers the splatters of red over her brand-new lavender lace dress, there's a huge shriek you could have heard over the loudest of LA traffic. She's so angry and upset. Not just at the dress being ruined, but she knows it was sabotage. The dress was nowhere near the kitchen, so someone had to have deliberately ruined it. She's practically in tears as she brings it out for everyone to see.

"Of course, her first thought was me. But my face was a picture of calm and innocence. She insisted on checking my hands in case of any red on my fingers and anything in my bag but comes up empty both times.

'Even if I did dislike you, which I don't, I would never ruin a dress,' I said as I inspected it. 'And this is Dior. I'm almost as upset as you.'

"That convinces her, and Hannah apologises with genuine sincerity. 'I should never have accused you. I'm so sorry. I just dreamed of wearing this when I saw it a few weeks ago. And now, I have nothing as good as that.'

"With that, I go to the room and hand her the gift I had brought in earlier. 'You should open it,' I say warmly.

She's completely bemused but opens it, and her face is a picture as she sees the shimmering blue Dior dress I had gotten for her. She's so genuinely happy I can see tears in her eyes.

"'I was hoping you would wear it for the first time when you came to the Christmas trip with me, but you should wear it now. Don't let anyone see you, and then you can have your big entrance later on.'

"'This is perfect!' she squeals and gives me a big hug. I hadn't wanted to get her anything so nice, but my mother had insisted it would be the classy thing to do. And seeing Hannah's heartfelt reaction, I was glad I listened to her. I've never been hugged by anyone like that before. It was like it melted the ice for both of us. As I helped her get into the dress upstairs, she apologised for not taking into account my feelings when organising her party and offered to let me borrow some accessories from her wardrobe. I said I shouldn't have made her birthday party feel so competitive and for the first time, I saw her as someone who could be my best friend. We had so much in common, it had taken us a while to sort things out, but now things were going to be just fine."

"You really were happy she was happy?" asked a sceptical Eric.

"It's hard to believe considering how I'd felt a few minutes earlier, but I really was," answered Madison. And despite everyone staring at the equipment, it was clear Madison was telling the truth. "You have no idea how tiring it was being the most popular girl in school. Everyone desperate for you to like them. Everyone copying everything you do, say and wear and eat. Being followed around in the hope of having their credibility increased. When Hannah hugged me, I realised we could be best friends. And I think she realised it too."

"So, what happened next?" said a sad-looking Eric.

"Well, having hidden the ketchup sachets in the girl's bag. I wasn't planning on anyone finding out. But while I was helping Hannah put on her new dress, her family had made everyone empty out their bags and purses. And that's when they saw the two ketchup sachets."

"With your new-found kindness, had you considered removing the ketchup sachets from that innocent girl's bag?" said Eric, staring Madison right in the eyes.

"You know, I've wondered that a lot over the years, especially with what happened after," responded Madison after considering the question in great detail. "I honestly don't know. I mean, I didn't want her to get caught, but at the time, she wasn't entirely innocent to me. I'd heard her make a joke at my expense when she thought I couldn't hear her, and I know from several people she had mimicked my voice as a joke. I know it's not much, but at the time I was unhappy with her."

"You still haven't answered me," said Eric with a smile, but with the firmness of someone not to be messed with.

"I never put it at the top of the bag. I only wanted to send a message to her. I wouldn't have told on her. But I couldn't risk being near her bag so no, the answer was, I wouldn't have tried to get to it. But it was more than that. The dress thing had been resolved. I wasn't even thinking about it. I thought it would all be forgotten about, which was incredibly naïve."

"So then what happened?"

"When we heard the commotion, we both ran down, even though we hadn't finished getting ready. That's when we both saw all the bags emptied and everyone surrounding this girl.

"What was her name? said the interviewer, with a dignified determination. "I think it's time we recognise her properly."

"You're sure she'd want to be named?"

"It's important," responded Eric emphatically.

"It was Fiona Appleby."

"So, go on."

So Fiona looks astonished and upset and can't think why the ketchup sachets are in her bag," continues Madison. "'I don't even eat ketchup,' says Fiona. 'I'm allergic. My face goes really red.'

"She's denying it, but of course, it doesn't look good for her.

"'I'm really disappointed in you Fiona,' says Hannah. 'Why would you do such a horrid thing? I thought you were my friend.'

"Fiona protests her innocence, but realising that her pleading won't get anywhere, she stops crying and decides to go on the attack. 'Someone has framed me. I mean, say it had been me, why would I leave the evidence in my own bag?'

"It's a valid point, and it does get us thinking.

"'Yeah, but it was at the bottom,' reasoned Hannah. 'You probably didn't think your bag would get checked. Besides, you probably didn't have time to hide it.'

"Which is again perceptive," continues Madison. "So that's when Fiona starts trying to work out who it was. Logically, it should be me. But Hannah and I are getting on so well, and me having such a Poker face rules it out. Or it could have been that I still had a lot of clout, and they were too nervous to challenge me. Or maybe that they thought I wasn't the type to get my hands dirty. Whatever it was, I was in the clear."

"So you weren't nervous?" asked a curious Eric.

"I rarely get nervous," said Madison. "At least outwardly. But I knew there was nothing they could use against me. And destroying a dress was so unlike me. Even now, I'm amazed I did it."

"Did you do anything to help defend Fiona or calm the situation?" asks Eric.

"There was nothing I could do," admitted an embarrassed Madison. "Things were too inflamed. If I had got involved, it would have been awkward and suspicious. I just assumed things would die down anyhow. I mean, there was no evidence. No one had seen anything, and Fiona did look genuinely bewildered, so I'm sure a lot of the girls there did believe her."

"So then what happened?"

"Hannah calmed down. It was helped by everyone telling her how excited they were to see her in the new dress only I had seen, and I think in fairness, she had to know that there was a good chance that Fiona was innocent. So Hannah made a dignified speech saying that someone had obviously wanted to ruin her big day, but she wasn't going to let that stop her. So Fiona stayed, Hannah took some photos in her new blue dress, and we all moved to the BBQ area.

"The plan was to open the presents first, but Hannah's parents thought it best to go into the garden, listen to some music and relax a little by the pool. The celebrity chef was sorting out a BBQ and definitely wasn't the type to be rushed.

"What we hadn't noticed was that while Hannah had calmed down, Fiona hadn't. She was still angry at being accused and knowing that someone had framed her. She later admitted that she had wanted an apology, like I had been given. That was incredibly unrealistic. Even if you ignored our different social statuses, she had been caught with the smoking gun in her bag as it were. At the time, I felt she was lucky not to have been thrown out under the circumstances. I still think that."

"That is interesting. I'm not sure I agree. Did no one notice Fiona's anger? How obvious was it?"

"Not at all. The thing was, she wasn't one of the more popular girls there. If it wasn't for the incident with the ketchup, I'm not sure anyone would really have remembered her being there. One of the shyer girls admitted later that she could sense something but was too nervous to interrupt the main group talking. To be honest, we were all excited that this TV chef was going to be cooking us a gourmet BBQ. Then we'd see Hannah open the presents, watch a film, play some games and then have our own dish specially prepared."

"And then it happened?"

"It turns out it had only been ten minutes since we moved outside, but it felt far longer. We were all getting hungry, but after what had happened to the dress, Hannah's mother was fitting us with these elegant bibs and had banned any sauce for the burgers, much to the disgust of the celebrity chef.

"That's probably what distracted us from the argument that was building between Fiona and the shy girl who had been studying her. Fiona in her paranoid state had assumed that the shy girl...

"Does this shy girl have a name?" asks the amiable host.

"I wouldn't know," responded the well-dressed blonde as she tried not to look down at the floor. "She wasn't important at all before this story."

"Ok, so continue," said Eric, trying not to sound resigned.

"So, what starts off as a quiet disagreement soon descends into a loud screaming match. Then there's pushing and screaming, and before anyone can do anything, they are properly going at it."

"You could have stopped it, though," interrupted Eric. "Were you tempted to say something at that point?"

"It never occurred to me," answered Madison, perhaps quicker than she intended to. "I'd just made a new best friend. Why would I ruin it just to stop two unimportant girls fighting? That's how I saw it then. If I'd known what was going to happen, of course. But life doesn't work like that."

The host looked down at his notes before slowly looking back up at Madison. "Describe what happened next as much as you remember."

"Well, the celebrity chef was in the kitchen being calmed down by Hannah's mum. He didn't understand why they wanted his burgers without sauce. Like Rachmaninov without a piano, he yelled. Like Messi with a blindfold. Then, the two girls started screaming and actually slapping each other and grappling. A few of the other girls tried to intervene, but unfortunately, that didn't stop them. And Hannah, who had been replying to a birthday message on her phone, was caught off-guard. She stood up to find out where the noise was coming from, unaware that the two girls and those trying to stop her had been bumbling towards her. She was caught off balance and then knocked hard."

There was a long pause as Madison's voice wavered. "If she'd landed anywhere other than the grill, it would have been fine. The garden was so big. And there was a pool. Statistically, it was like a needle in a haystack. I can still hear the scream just after her face touched the metal."

The crowd had been quiet all through the description. But the mention of the grill and the scream made it more visual, more real, and there were audible gasps. They could picture the horror, and they felt sick.

"I can't even begin to imagine," said Eric quietly.

"That scream," said an ashen Madison. "And the smell."

"So what happened after that?" asked Eric slowly.

"Just panic. The thing was, she didn't just touch the grill, she landed on it really hard, so at one point, it was stuck. I threw her into the pool, which helped, I think. Someone had called an ambulance, and they arrived soon after, and she was drugged to stop the pain. She was taken to the burns unit, and her parents went with her. The nanny took charge of us but didn't really say too much, only that we couldn't leave yet. She had a sweet disposition and wouldn't have been able to handle us if we'd all been unruly, but everyone was so traumatised, most of us barely said a word."

"There was nothing in the news at the time," said a solemn Eric. "I would have remembered a story like that. Researching it, I couldn't find anything either. Why was that?"

"Everyone was sworn to a non-disclosure. A draft was hurriedly written up by a lawyer at her father's firm, who had been working with him at the time of the accident. Before he left, Hannah's father insisted he didn't want news of this getting out under any circumstances. No one could leave until it had been signed. Most signed their names without reading a word. Just took a signed copy with them, as they were so desperate to be out of here. I mean these were ten-year-old girls signing without their parents present, so legally it was pretty worthless. But he was so intense and insistent on the punishments if we didn't, that we would have agreed to anything."

There was a gap of several moments while the enormity and horror of what happened was digested. Eric had already read about it before, but it seemed so much worse hearing it with the slow build-up. "So, what happened to Hannah?" he asked in the most sympathetic voice he could come up with.

"While they were waiting for the ambulance, her father reassured her that the best surgeons in the world would be flown over to work on her. I didn't actually know which hospital she went to. I tried to reach out, but the texts showed up as unread, and her phone went straight to voicemail. After a while, the newer messages came back as number unrecognised. When I went to her house, it was blocked by heavy security, and I'm not even sure my visit was passed on."

"What would you have said to her if you had been able to?"

"I'd have said sorry," said Madison, looking genuinely contrite. "It was just a petty squabble that got out of hand. It was a horrible accident. And I would have told her my part in it. The guilt ate away at me for weeks. I could barely eat or sleep and had to see a child psychologist. It was a horrible time. But whatever my pain was, I knew the agony for Hannah would have been worse."

"What happened to the two girls that had been fighting?"

"They were quietly told to leave. While their parents were able to afford the school's fees and they hadn't done anything wrong on school grounds, it was felt best for everyone if they went somewhere different. As far as I know, they went to two different places and never spoke to each other after that."

Eric paused as several questions came to mind. "And you never saw or heard of Hannah again?"

"No."

"Have you ever thought about her and whether you would reach out to her given the chance?"

"Yes, although it's not my decision," said Madison in a quiet voice. "She's the one who suffered most that day."

With that, Selina shocked everyone by coming onto the stage, in full view of all the cameras. Without saying anything, she removed all the cables connected to Madison. The heavy machinery was moved away.

"You answered questions relating to all four names," said Selina with cool efficiency. "As promised, you can now take home your money and your trophy. Thank you for your time and professionalism, Eric."

Before Madison or Eric had a chance to answer, Selina emptied all the names in the glass container and threw them into a large bin she had brought along. She gave Madison a set of matches. "Why don't you do the honours?"

Madison smiled awkwardly and then lit the fire three times. Once just didn't seem enough. As she stared at the flames that soon burst out, Selina handed her the trophy and the cheque for the money and pointed her to the exit.

"It's all over," she said, clapping her hands in emphasis. "You made it. You can now do or say whatever you want when interviewed. I'd just remind you, like I have with the other five, that we have everything on tape in case things get too nasty. And we have the best lawyers in town."

Madison was exhausted and disinterested in thinking about the future. The last four names had made her think about the past far more than she had ever intended to. She really was ashamed of her own behaviour and how little excuse she had for any of it.

As Selina went to walk off, Madison tapped her shoulder to stop her.

"I've answered all your questions today, and you brought up a lot of things I didn't want anyone else to know about. What was the point of all this?"

Selina smiled. "I wanted to tell you, but the crowd voted that you should only find out if you asked, so I went with their call. But now you've asked the question, I can answer you honestly. The crowd tonight is different to the ones before the five challenges. You'll have noticed we removed the audio barrier, which meant you could hear the crowd when they shouted at you tonight. While those before were carefully chosen strangers, a select number tonight is connected to at least one name written down within that glass cylinder. Some directly, some indirectly. You answered four of them, but there were another 14 names to choose from.

"And each of those 18 names was unhappy with me?" said Madison, astonished by the high number.

"Hugely. But it wasn't just you. Within the people in the crowd were people affected negatively by at least one of the six of you. Some were unpleasant interactions; some were left with lasting damage or having to deal with those who suffered greatly from being around you. In some cases, emotional, and yes, in more extreme cases, physical damage, too. A great number wanted revenge, others wanted to give you the chance to see if you had changed and were sorry. That's why the punishments reflected that. Some of the group have done very well for themselves, owning major businesses and having loving marriages and families. For others, life has been a great struggle. But between them, they came up with the idea and pooled their resources to cover everything.

"So does the crowd know who those 100+ affected people within the crowd are?" wondered Madison.

"No, which is just as the group wanted it. No one knows who those 108 people are, only the people themselves know if they are one of them."

"Is Hannah one of them?"

"She is, though she goes under a different name, and you wouldn't recognise her."

Madison looked at Selina for a long time before saying anything.

"'Hannah' has gone on to have a good life," added Selina. "She married, has children and is happy. She's happy."

Madison looked at her, and it was clear there was something she wasn't sure whether to ask.

"No, too much has happened since then, and she moved on a long time ago," said Selina in a kind voice, knowing what the question would be. "But she has forgiven you. She admitted she was rooting for you not to get chosen whenever the wheel was spinning. She's in the crowd, but we thought she should leave before the burning ceremony. Everyone mentioned in the story agreed to having their names being mentioned. The other girl's name was Jackie Filbert."

With that, Selina threw down the curtain, and Madison could see the thousands looking at her. Even though she knew she wouldn't recognise Hannah, she still looked for anyone that might be a relative of hers. What she did notice was the range of faces, and every possible emotion you could imagine. Content, serene, distracted, sad, wistful, angry, sympathetic, disappointed, anxious, jealous, confused. She knew most of them weren't even connected to her. They had been fallouts from the other five, but she felt responsible for them. If they were anything like the four people she had just answered in detail about, then they would have suffered a great deal. And she was ashamed. She really had been a rotten person.

Madison picked up her trophy, still the first she had ever won. She hadn't had a chance to hold it properly or have any photos taken. She looked at it for a few moments and then threw it emphatically in the bin. The flames had faltered significantly, and Madison looked at it triumphantly. A large weight had been lifted off her shoulders, and she felt more energised than she had ever felt in her entire life.

She picked up the envelope and gave it to a surprised Selina, who for the first time since the process had been genuinely taken aback. "It's theirs," said the heiress. "Please ensure the 108 people share the $7.2 million equally."

The crowd was just as surprised, but Madison didn't look back to gauge their reaction. She still had no watch, but she knew whatever it said, it was time for her to leave. She had no idea if the other five were the same as when they entered the competition, but she didn't feel like she was.

As she collected her things, she knew she was finally a free woman again with a more enlightened view of the world and the people in it. Walking out into natural sunshine for what seemed like the first time in months, Madison worked out what $7.2 million divided by 108 was and smiled. For what they had all suffered, it wasn't much, but it was a start. It was a start.

THE END

Printed in Dunstable, United Kingdom

66807995R00107